MOONTIDE

Mary Greenwood

HAWKEYE
PUBLISHING

First published in Australia in 2023 by Hawkeye Publishing.

Cover Design by Eli Southward

A catalogue record of this book is available from the National Library of Australia.

ISBN 9780645714968

Proudly printed in Australia.

www.hawkeyepublishing.com.au
www.hawkeyebooks.com.au

Praise for *Moontide*

'A tale of longing, lyrically told. A world where shape-changers test the boundary between the animal and human. A story that savagely sings of loss and redemption. This young adult fantasy novel is both beautiful and compelling.'
Miriam Wei Wei Lo, Poet.

'An exciting and powerfully written debut fantasy about family secrets and the outsider's need for fellowship and belonging in the face of superstitious fear and prejudice. Mary Greenwood's world-building is strong and her characters are engaging.'
Deborah Burroughs, Author.

'An exciting read, full of engaging and strong characters. Especially the girls!'
T. C. Shelley, Author.

'A well-woven story that is engaging and rich in folklore. Greenwood is a talented storyteller and by the end of this novel you cannot help but look at the sea and wonder.'
Khaiah Thomson, Author.

'Moontide is a haunting fantasy, a dark and beautiful fairytale that draws on old folklore and rich mythologies to weave an intricate tapestry of rights and wrongs, pasts and futures, choices and curses. A world which crystallises the conflicts of self vs nature, self vs self, and asks if there is any forgiveness in either. A novel with a well-deserved victory to its name.'
Nita Delgado, Editor.

DEDICATION

My first fruits to the Author of Life.

1

The first thing you must realise is just how cold it was.

Frost crisscrossed in snowflake patterns over the stones scattered across the grasslands. Ice ridged the long grass, so it feathered stark white against the charcoal morning.

The second thing is that the moon had only recently set, having coasted across the night like a lantern on a still pond. In its wake, Fiadh had shivered into her own mind, had feebly risen to her red-sore feet and smoothed the coarse fur of her wolf pelt over her milk skin, with no more idea of where she was than if she had walked in her sleep.

And lastly, bear in mind that I had been abandoned for years. My crystal and glass crown was only a shattered prism atop my grey stone spire. No one had set foot within me since they had unleashed fire from my hearth and strewn it across my floors, since they had torn father from child and flung him down into the raging sea. Since they had snuffed my light and cursed me to watch ships wreck and tides wage war, helpless to save the lives I had been built to save.

Fiadh couldn't have known this when she beat in my weathered door and fell, sprawling, in a cloud of ash and dust. She did not spare it a thought as she floundered to the hearth, fighting the trembling in her frost-nipped fingers, to heap brittle wood and tinder from the inglenook into the fireplace.

But, as you surely now understand, we cannot hold this against her. When she was finally able to strike a spark into the kindling, and smoky warmth blossomed within me, I forgave her. I welcomed her.

I recognised her. Her hands and mouth stained with blood, her pinched and narrow frame, the dry sobs that rasped in her throat. I recognised an equal in shame and brokenness.

Fiadh, listen. I have a story to share. Will you hear it howling in my eaves? Feel it gusting down my chimney with a fine mist of rain? See it in the gossamer ghosts flitting over the dust and ashes? Scent it on the salt wind that wails with the voices of the lost?

I can only hope you will.

⌘

Fiadh fumbled her flints back into the cloth pouch knotted around her neck. She leaned as close to the newborn flame as she could, holding her palms out to the snapping heat.

Her hands were dyed a dull red.

They were chafed, the skin around her nail beds peeling, but Fiadh knew the blood wasn't her own. She curled her fingers, inspecting her ragged nails. Crimson sickles had crusted beneath them. She ran her tongue over her teeth and tasted the familiar tang of blood.

The first time, she had screamed. She had spat and retched and screamed again. She had clawed at the wolf pelt that clung to her as a second skin, trying desperately to cast it off. But by then, the curse had sunk its teeth too deeply into her. The curse she had fostered, despite her father's warnings to use the pelt sparingly, to use it only when in dire need. Lest the wolf wake.

But there was no use in screaming now. Fiadh drew her knees up and buried her face in them, trying not to think about what must have happened. What she must have done.

'Stay strong, wild one,' Fiadh breathed, her underused voice a croak. 'Stay safe. We will find each other again.' She knew the shape of her father's words, but they had lost the echo of his voice.

Unfurling her wiry body, she pushed herself to her feet. They twinged painfully as they took her weight, and she caught herself on the mantelpiece. Her eyes fell to the roughhewn shelf beneath her hand. It was decorated with tiny shells of pink, white and lilac, patterned around chips of mother-of-pearl.

Fiadh smiled at the small glimmer of beauty. Tentatively, she caressed the twining pattern. Her stained fingertips smudged reddish prints on the shells and plaster and she snatched her hand back. She frowned.

In the flickering firelight, she saw that the stones at the base of the mantelpiece were blackened. Her gaze trailed down to the floor, where the slate was similarly marred. A rug sprawled in singed tatters on the other side of the hearth. And now that the morning light was growing brighter, spilling into the room like ribbons of silver gauze, Fiadh saw more signs of the violence that had been wrought in this place.

Fire had licked its way around the room, long ago. Left the memory of its writhing etched on the stone walls, charred into the narrow door sulking in one corner, seared in the posts of a bed pushed up against the wall. It had even licked as high as the sloped ceiling, blackening the rafters above her head.

Fiadh pushed herself away from the fireplace, suddenly too warm. Squinting against the glare of the dawning sun, she shuffled to the latticed windows. They wrapped around a scullery nook that jutted from the curve of the eastern wall. Fiadh shoved a clutter of filthy crockery from the bench beneath them and hoisted herself up to reach the window latch. She fumbled with it until the warped wood of the frame gave, screeching as she shoved it free. A gust of chill air burst in and she leaned into it.

All at once, Fiadh knew she didn't want to stay here any longer. Something had happened within these walls, something cruel. A darkness beyond burned wood and stone lingered in this place. She shivered and rubbed her bare arms. No, she didn't want to stay here at all.

Fiadh slid off the bench, but as her tender feet touched the slate and her knees trembled, she realised she couldn't leave. Her body ached, her limbs heavy from a night of activity she didn't remember.

Supporting herself against the wall, she padded to the large bed opposite the fireplace, her hand sliding over rough stone and smooth plaster. A clothes chest squatted at the foot of the bed. She moved to skirt around it but stopped. The chest was perfect. The fire hadn't so much as licked its corners.

Fiadh knelt and brushed away the coating of dust that clung to the glossy wood. The chest had been carved with scenes of fishing boats and ocean creatures. Seals coiled beneath rocking boats, where fishermen hauled in their day's catch, playing just out of reach of their nets. The carvings were so detailed, so beautiful. They stirred a memory within her, of a story her father had once told her of selkies, those ethereal creatures that shed their seal skins to walk as humans on the shore. Fiadh wanted to reach out and touch one of the tiny seals – so lifelike she wouldn't have been surprised if they moved under her hand – but she remembered the blood dying her fingers and snatched them to her chest.

She stood up quickly. Too quickly. Clutching the bed's sturdy post, she fought a sudden wave of uneasiness she couldn't explain.

Just a few hours of sleep, she told herself. The mattress sagged in the middle, sheets rumpled from a night many years old. Fiadh collapsed onto the bed, upsetting a cloud of dust, and folded her aching frame into its meagre comfort.

Just a few hours of sleep.

Just a few hours…

A few hours in her own skin. And then the night would come and the wolf would run her ragged and drink its fill of blood.

Fiadh screwed her eyes shut against her painful thoughts, her frustrated grief.

The wind keened in the chimney, rousing a phantom voice. As she gave in to sleep, Fiadh heard a lullaby lilting faintly, on the cusp of her awareness. A lullaby she had never heard before.

But the lighthouse had heard it and the lighthouse remembered.

2

BRENNA pulled the bandage tight with a grunt, the coarse linen clenched between her teeth. Spitting the cloth out, she tied it off clumsily. She tossed the soiled rags she'd used to staunch her bleeding onto the table and leaned against it, breathing hard. When she hung her head, her mass of red curls cascaded over her pallid, sweaty face.

If it had been anyone else—

Brenna smacked her fist on the wood. The table shuddered.

If that wretched wolf had attacked anyone else, they wouldn't have needed to tend to themselves. No, they would've been offered help. The people who'd come running at her shrieks, who'd faltered when they saw her flaming hair, her despised face, would've fought to protect someone else. Anyone else.

Brenna knew the people of Sjavaba hated her. As they had her father. It wasn't enough, apparently, that he was dead. They watched her with the same scorn, the same fear, as if what her father had done had stained her too.

That was why she'd been alone in the twilit dark, scouring the skirts of the wood for firewood to bulk out her winter stores, rather than with the other young townsfolk retiring from the day's work. That was why she'd entered the once-great seaport from the southeast, where the tall walls crumbled to rubble, instead of the main northern gate that led to the town square, Sjavaba's beating heart. Why she'd slunk through the ruined district where no one else dared walk, feeling like a criminal in her own hometown.

Brenna hadn't heard the tread of the white wolf's paws as it followed her from the wood and across the grasslands. As it prowled in her wake, scenting her from afar. The tall wind-brushed grass had sighed and whispered its warnings in vain.

The first she'd known of approaching danger was the skitter of claws on uneven cobbles. The wolf's teeth slamming into her thigh, nail-sharp, ripping cloth and flesh. The force of its lunge knocking her forward.

The memory of the attack played like a pantomime behind her eyelids.

She'd fallen forward, the bundle of sticks flying from her arms and clattering on the cobbles. She'd screamed. Rolled onto her back, gasping when she saw the wolf that had her in its maw. Tried to kick it off, but her foot had skidded uselessly off its muzzle. Thunder had cracked overhead, loud enough to shudder the earth, as it had started to rain. The wolf had shaken its head, heat searing her flesh. She'd screamed again, shrieking for help. Releasing her thigh, the wolf had turned wild, amber eyes to meet her own. She'd thrown up her hands but hadn't been able to stop the reddened jaws from closing on her shoulder. Hot blood had pooled around its teeth and soaked her sleeve, pouring as libations onto the mud. Her screams had torn her throat raw, until they were nothing but silent gasps.

Shouts had echoed through the rush of rain and bellow of thunder. In a haze, Brenna had twisted to see. Red lantern light had flickered on the ruined walls, throwing back the shadows. Townsfolk! The people of Sjavaba were coming to save her. She had never been so relieved, so grateful!

A score of people had rounded the corner, brandishing torches. But when they'd seen Brenna, limp in the wolf's jaws, they'd stopped. Frozen in their tracks. Shock and revulsion had twisted their faces. None of them had moved to help. Brenna's crazed eyes had darted to each face, searching for any glimmer of kindness, any sign of pity.

None.

The wolf's snarl had reverberated through her flesh, the hair bristling down its back. It'd dropped her like a broken doll and sprung at the onlookers. They'd cried out, batted at it with their torches, scattering sparks. The wolf had whined and given up, bounding away, disappearing through the crooked alleys in a flash of white fur.

Even once the wolf had vanished, no one had approached to help her.

Brenna had hauled herself, excruciatingly, to her feet, fighting not to slip on the cobbles slick with rain and blood. Her vision had blurred, her hands shaking. The cluster of townsfolk had watched her warily, holding their torches out, as though she were another threat they might need to fend off. But she'd thrust her chin high and limped past them, followed by unfeeling eyes.

When she'd known she was out of sight, she'd sagged against the nearest wall, biting her tongue for daring to hope that anyone from this spiteful town would ever lift a finger for her.

Brenna swiped at her eyes. There was no use dwelling on it further. She'd long known where she stood with the people of Sjavaba. This reminder would just make it easier to leave them all behind.

Leaving the bowl of bloodied water, she limped around the table, bandages and torn clothes strewn across its uneven surface. It stood askew between a fireplace and the bolted front door. The hovel only had one other room, a scant bedchamber with water-stained plaster and a boarded window.

No one resented that she'd claimed the hovel for herself. It was one of the least-damaged houses in the southern district. The flood had failed to destroy it. It was fitting, as she knew the townsfolk said, that she dwelt surrounded by the ruins her father had caused. On the outskirts, far away from the rest of the town and its people. What harm could she do there?

Brenna moved across the dim room and ducked under the curtain she'd strung across the bedchamber's empty doorframe. She lowered herself to the floor beside her clothes chest, her injured leg sticking awkwardly out before her.

On their way to unlatch the clasp, her fingertips traced the roiling waves her father had carved into the wood. It was one of the only things she'd salvaged from her childhood home. A gift from the time when her father had been pleased to have a daughter.

She flipped the lid open and rummaged for clean clothes. In the years since she lost her father, she'd outgrown her girlhood garments. He'd bought her dresses embroidered with strange animals and tunics dyed in colours no native cloth had seen. Merchants had sold him glass bead necklaces and rings cast from foreign ores. Pretty gifts for Brenna and her mother, to demonstrate his love.

Yes, she had outgrown them.

Now the chest held homespun tunics of grey, brown, or dull red. She dressed herself carefully, wincing as she worked her injured arm into her shirtsleeve and struggled into trousers that agitated her torn thigh.

Brenna pushed from the floor with painful effort and made her way back to the front room. She collected her father's coat from where she'd discarded it on the kitchen table. It was overlarge and smelled of oil and salt. One of the shoulders was ripped and several buttons were missing. She draped it over her shoulders, readying herself to step out into the cold predawn air.

She hadn't slept. Weariness crusted the corners of her eyes. Her injuries throbbed. But she wouldn't stay in that hovel of a house and steep in frustration and pain. She knew what waited for her at the bottom of that spiral.

Until her thigh healed, she would need a walking staff and medicine to protect her wounds. She'd have to go into the town proper for those, to the apothecary's medicine house. She gritted her teeth at the thought of tossing her money away to people who distrusted and scorned her.

But she'd do what was needed to heal, to survive. Then, when the winter ended, she would be done with Sjavaba.

And its people.

3

FIADH woke with the lullaby still lurking in her ears. It was in another language, deep and viscous, husky and light.

She groaned, her body aching, and sat up on the mattress. Frowning, she kneaded her ears, trying to dissipate the prowling voice. But it persisted.

It wasn't just a memory, or an illusion. She could *hear* it.

Fiadh sprung off the bed. Her feet skidded over the floor, her hands coming down to brace her body. She tossed her head back and forth, straining her ears, sniffing the air. The lighthouse smelled as it had before, of dank wood, salt, and soot. No one else *could* be here. No one moved in the scullery nook or sat by the fireplace. The room was as empty and dim as it had been when she'd first sprawled into it. Not even the cobwebs stirred.

Cautiously, Fiadh raised herself from all fours and crept away from the bed. As she crossed the room, the singing faded, her ears ringing with the sudden silence.

Fiadh exhaled and the tension eased from her shoulders. She swept her eyes around the room once more, turning slowly on the spot—

A woman sat on the bed.

Fiadh froze.

She looked like no woman Fiadh had ever seen. Her skin was dappled silver and fawn, her hair cascading to the floor in a rippling waterfall that splashed about her bare feet. A simple shift fell loosely

11

over her plump body. She rocked on the bed, crushing a bundle of blankets to her bosom. Her lips moved in song, her long-lashed eyes far away.

Fiadh blinked and rubbed her eyes, but the vision remained. She licked her dry lips. Took a step closer.

The woman jolted. Her fingers clawed, clutching the bundle tightly, protectively. She leapt from the bed and spun around. Her round black eyes found Fiadh's—

And she vanished.

Fiadh gasped. Her hand flailed for the mantelshelf to stop herself from sinking to the floor.

What was that? Fiadh thought, breathing hard. *What* was *that?* Who *was that?*

She staggered to the middle of the room. No visions. No sounds. The spectre had disappeared. But why had she seen it? Why had she heard it? Had she really? Had it been only a waking dream?

Fiadh shook her head. She didn't want to know. She'd dabbled with things beyond her understanding before. As she clasped her hands over the wolf pelt, the coarse white fur rustled under her touch. She wanted no part in whatever this new magic was.

Fiadh spun on the ball of her foot and ran, kicking up dust and ash as she bolted for the front door. She wrenched it open. Icy wind and a light flurry of snow gusted in, the grasslands splayed out before her, dusted with fresh snowflakes. She hesitated only a second before darting out into the open.

The frozen earth nipped her feet. Tall grass stung her calves. But she didn't look back at the lighthouse, afraid she would see something, some*one*, staring back at her from its broken facade.

Fiadh pitched forward, tumbling down a hill she'd missed in her panic. Her body crushed a path through the ice-feathered grass. She rolled to a stop and sat up shakily. Shivered. Poked her head above the grass to take stock of her location.

The dark shadow of a wood crouched a furlong to her right. Black branches twisted against the white of the snow and the grey of the glowering sky. The forest spanned the horizon, east to west, in an undulating line, following the rise and dip of the grasslands. To her left, the hills swept down into a valley. Nestled in the dip of the land, between the wood and the ocean, was a town.

Fiadh clambered to her feet and craned her neck. The town had been built right up to the water. She could make out a network of paths, houses, shops, and courtyards. Towards the sea, the tiled roofs and brick walls gave way to blackened ruins. It looked as if charcoal had been smeared across a painting, blurring the neat lines of the manmade structures with the wild, choppy curve of the coast.

Fiadh sucked her lip. She had no right to go there, to brush shoulders with ordinary people. Not when she had cast aside her own humanity to don another hide. It was too dangerous. *She* was too dangerous.

But she didn't have a choice. Her legs shook, her bare arms covered in goosebumps. Hunger gnawed at her stomach. And the snow was falling more quickly by the minute. If she took refuge in the hills or the woods, it would only be a matter of time before the winter claimed her. She couldn't allow that.

'Stay strong, wild one,' she murmured. She set her shoulders and struck out towards the town. 'I will find you again, *Pabbi*. I will live to find you again.'

⌘

A beaten-earth road cut through the grasslands in a crooked line, from the woods to the town's front gates. Fiadh stopped at the foot of the lighthouse hill, wary of stepping onto the road and into full view of anyone who might be watching. As she crouched in the long grass, the wind teased her hair across her cheek. She raised a hand to brush it back and saw the dried blood crusted on her fingers. Hurriedly, she gathered fistfuls of fresh snow, cupping her hands together until the powder melted. She scrubbed at her hands, mouth, and neck, gritting her teeth against the cold nipping her raw skin.

Once she was satisfied the marks of the wolf's violence no longer stained her, Fiadh crept cautiously onto the road. Her heart cringed in her chest as she moved closer to the town. She sniffed the wind. It smelled of salt and wood smoke, fresh-baked bread, sweat and dirt. It smelled familiar.

Cobbles dotted the frozen earth of the road as it neared the town. Fiadh padded softly through the gates, ears alert, eyes wide. It had been a long time since she'd last entered a settlement. She'd kept to woodlands and the occasional farming estate or charcoal burner's hut for the better part of the past two years. Even so, she didn't think it had been long enough to forget what they were like.

She paused in the shadow of the wall, fingertips brushing the stone, anchoring her in place. She'd expected to see people. Towns were packed with people, bustling, milling, working, clanging, stomping, speaking, and shouting over one another so that the whole place hummed and buzzed with noise, like a hive. Her father had never liked visiting towns. She could picture the tension in his shoulders when they'd had to go to market to sell pelts he had hunted for.

But there was no hive-hum here.

A few people clustered in the paved courtyard just inside the gate. They wore heavy coats and shawls against the chill wind and stood cramped in the doorway of a tall brick building. They were in rapt conversation, shooting furtive looks into the courtyard. Fiadh edged closer, ears pricked.

'The keeper's daughter, yes,' an older woman hissed, clutching the folds of her headscarf.

'Did it attack anyone else?' asked a broad-shouldered man.

The woman shook her head. 'It turned on the people who found her, but they beat it off.'

A willowy woman with a sour mouth sniffed sharply. 'They shouldn't have interfered at all!'

'What do you mean, my dear?'

'Why, think! A white wolf. Its attack was clearly a reckoning. Even the feywalkers want to be rid of that keeper's brat. We should never have let her fester here so long.'

White wolf.

Fiadh's face flushed hot, her body cold.

'Shh!' the man said. 'It's unwise to invoke them.' He glanced around the courtyard and gasped. His companions stiffened, following his gaze.

They had seen her.

Run. The wolf is fast.

She didn't move. Her legs were weak.

The wolf will carry you far away. It will protect you.

It hurt someone. It might have *killed.*

So leave. You can't be here. How dare you be here!

Fiadh sank to her knees. The man caught her by the arms, heaving her upright. He supported her weight and looked her over. The two women were right behind him, fussing nervously.

Don't do that. Fiadh stammered an apology and struggled to pull away. *Don't pity me. Don't look at me like I'm some harmless child.*

But he drowned out her protests with concern. 'You're frozen! Poor thing. You look like you've been through hell.' He wrapped an arm around her shoulders. 'I'll take her to Yuel,' he told the two hovering women.

Fiadh squirmed. *Don't! Please! I've done enough!*

But he held her firmly, kindly, and guided her through the streets the wolf's teeth and claws had defiled.

4

BRENNA leaned against a wall, her face twisted in pain. Snow-laden clouds darkened the streets, despite the hour of the morning. The lamps were still lit. They illuminated her fiery hair and well-known figure as she hobbled up the thoroughfare. She couldn't ignore the sidelong looks, the too-loud mutterings, of those she passed, but pretended not to notice them.

Resting her back against the wall, she eased her weight off her injured leg. She touched her thigh gingerly, wincing at the spike of pain. The leg of her trousers felt damp, and when she drew her hand away, she saw that blood had seeped through the bandages, a blossoming dark stain. Grimacing, she pushed herself up and staggered on.

Her foot caught in a hole between cobblestones. She lurched forward and just managed to steady herself, cursing under her breath.

Sjavaba's streets had seen better years. When the harbour had been a bustling centre of industry and trade, when it had accommodated merchants and travellers on their way to the larger ports in the north, the town had ample money to spend on keeping its streets clean and well maintained.

Brenna remembered her semi-frequent visits to Sjavaba with her father as a child. She remembered walking at his side, her small hand firmly held in his big calloused one, struggling to keep pace with his long-legged strides. The cobbles had been washed clean and glistening sun-gold after the rains. Townsfolk had dressed in fashions imported

16

from distant shores, paying keen attention to any new styles worn by their exotic visitors. Shop awnings had been adorned with garlands from aromatic trees, so the streets smelled fresh and alive, earthy and sweet, even as the sea breeze brought the pungent salt-and-fish scent of the fishermen's catch.

Back then, the southern district had been Sjavaba's central hub. Brenna's father had spent much time at the docks, speaking jovially with sailors and fishermen. Brenna would slip away from him as he prowled the promenade. She would wend through the milling throng of briny workers until she reached the end of the boardwalk. She'd run down its weathered steps and across the damp sands. Kick off her boots and jump into the cold, lapping sea. Lean down to cup her hands in the grey-green water. Feel the tide drag at her ankles, as if beckoning her to wade further, to sink deeper, into its icy darkness.

Before the southern district had been destroyed.

The last time she'd walked on the black sands, the filthy ocean had lapped sluggishly around her legs, like a beast overfull with debris from ship and shore, with the lives it'd swallowed. And her father hadn't been striding across the promenade, laughing among friends and strangers. The tide had spat him onto the waterlogged boardwalk, his red hair straggled with seaweed, body pierced and broken, eyes glassy in death.

Clasping her weeping leg, Brenna hauled herself into the new town square. The main centres of business and governance had been relocated to Sjavaba's north since the devastation of the southern district.

Brenna swept her gaze contemptuously over the graceless buildings. She turned up the collar of her coat and shambled down the broad street that led to Yuel's medicine house. The shop had a narrow facade, shallow, uneven steps leading to a heavy black door. A single lantern hung beside it, casting a weak halo of light.

She puckered her mouth in distaste, but ascended the steps, clutching the rusted railing. As she raised her right arm to knock, she flinched, the movement agitating her wound. She let out a frustrated snarl and shifted her weight, pounding the door with her left fist.

'*Apótekari!*' she shouted.

The handle rattled as she leaned back against the railing. The door creaked inward and a young man appeared in the gap. The apothecary's assistant was a contrast of angular features and loose, relaxed mannerisms. He tossed his silky black hair out of his eyes and arched a brow at her.

'Speak of the devil.'

Brenna wrinkled her nose. 'Charming as always, Bo.' She moved to push past him, but he draped himself against the jamb, blocking the entrance.

'I wouldn't,' he said, a crisp edge to his voice.

'What's that supposed to mean? Look, I'm bleeding and I need the *apótekari*'s help. Are you going to let me in?'

Bo blinked slowly, expression suggesting he was giving Brenna what she asked to spite her. 'As you wish,' he said, stepping back and pulling the door wide open. Brenna felt a twinge of unease but forced her way forward.

The apothecary's store was high-ceilinged and panelled with black wood. Rows of drawers of assorted size, all labelled in white chalk, filled the wall behind the counter at the far end of the room. Shelves lined the left wall. Tall orange candles had been placed on the tops of cabinets and on spindly candelabras, their light glancing eerily off the glossy black surfaces. The right side of the room was partitioned with a folding screen of varnished wood and ink-brushed paper. Brenna knew that behind it, the apothecary had set up a number of cots for his patients.

She blinked in surprise. The store was crowded with people, fighting for elbow room in the cramped space. They pressed in towards the service counter, speaking over one another in an aggressive babble. The floorboards juddered underfoot, the crush of bodies blocking the counter from view. She couldn't even see the apothecary. Bo closed the door behind her, his fingertips lingering on the wood as the latch clipped into place.

'What's this about?' Brenna asked, raising her voice to be heard above the noise. 'Is there a sickness?'

'Last chance,' Bo said. 'If I were you, I'd—'

A screeching cry pierced the clamour. 'She's here! The keeper's brat is here!'

The hubbub died at once.

Brenna was accustomed to the spite with which the townsfolk regarded her. But even she was taken aback by their faces. Their anger and fear. Their bared teeth as they turned. As those closest to her broke away from the crowd and advanced on her—

'Wait!' she cried. She tried to back away but staggered into Bo. A command rang out – *Hold her!'* – and Bo's hands leapt to grab her arms. His long fingers cinched around her injured bicep. She yelled in pain and squirmed in his grasp, caught his stiff-lipped expression. Yet he wasn't even looking at her, but over her, eyes glazed.

'What have I done?' she demanded, her voice shrill. 'I haven't *done* anything!'

'How dare you show your face?' a woman shouted, marching up to where Brenna sagged in Bo's grip. She raised her arm and struck Brenna fully across the cheek. A cheer rang out with the blow.

'There's no help for you here!' roared a man's gravelly voice.

'Even the feywalkers think you've lived too long!'

'Keeper's brat!'

'Curse-bearer!'

Brenna's heels scraped uselessly against the floorboards. She couldn't break away, couldn't break free from their attack. 'I'm not!'

The woman struck Brenna's other cheek. Pinpoints of light sparked across her vision, the room spinning around her.

Desperate to get away, Brenna flung her head back, cracking it into Bo's chin. He grunted and dropped her, clutching at his face. She scrabbled away. Her back hit the wall and she found herself cornered.

She flung her arms over her head, as her attackers surged towards her, were upon her—

'Stop, stop, *stop!*'

Brenna's heart pounded against her ribs. But no one grabbed her. No one struck her. Even their shouts had subsided. She peered between her arms to see who had saved her.

The crowd milled uncertainly and parted. The grey-haired apothecary shuffled out from their midst, a stern expression on his weathered face. His eyes narrowed as he regarded the scene over the rim of his small round spectacles.

'I will not have th-this *violence* in my store,' Yuel said firmly. 'I do not sell herbs, poultices or trinkets for warding off imagined spectres. None of you are ailing in a way I can treat. So if you're going to make such a-a ruckus, I will have to ask you to leave. At once.' Without waiting for a response, he turned and approached Brenna.

From her prone position, Yuel looked just as fierce as those who'd attacked her. But he knelt and laid a hand on her shoulder. His gaze flickered over her – not in real kindness, rather with simple professional interest. But Brenna welcomed even a dispassionate examination after the hostility she'd just faced.

'Come to a cot and I will see to you in a moment,' he said.

A roar of protest broke out behind them. Yuel snapped his head around. 'Now that's enough!' he barked. 'All of you, out! I cannot tend to real patients with such a-a *commotion* in my store. Bo, make yourself useful.'

'*Afi*, she's the one they're—'

'I'm no fool, Bo. I know who she is. Do as I tell you.' The old physician stood up and doddered behind the folding screens.

Brenna waited warily as Bo ushered the crowd out of the shop. A tawny-haired man spat at her feet as he passed. A gaggle of young children clutched each other, giggling nervously behind their hands. She turned away, letting her curls veil her face. When the last of them had left, Bo shot her a look that was trying to be imperious but had rather a twist of distaste about the lip, then tossed his head and strode to the service counter. Keeping an eye on him, Brenna struggled to her feet and limped after Yuel.

Three short cots stood behind the screen, made up with crisp grey sheets. Between each stood a small cabinet. Yuel bent before one, rummaging through and setting a collection of items – bandages, spools of twine, a needle, a tiny bottle of brown glass – on its top. Brenna's stomach twisted.

'*Apótekari*, I don't need anything like that. I just came for a walking staff...'

'No, no, no,' Yuel said, without looking up. 'I've heard the story over a dozen times this morning. The wolf very nearly killed you, by all accounts. I'll take care of you properly.'

'I can't afford that.'

Yuel straightened up and fixed her with stern eyes. Eyes that seemed to look beyond what was before them. 'Consider the price already paid, Idunn's daughter.'

Brenna's throat tightened. She opened her mouth, but couldn't form words. With a weak nod, she sank onto the nearest cot, her mind and body still thrilling with nerves.

Yuel clicked his tongue and shut the cabinet door sharply. He moved around the foot of her cot.

'*Apótekari*...' she started, but he shuffled around the screen before she could ask her question. Sighing, she leaned her head against the headboard, staring at the high ceiling.

'So, you survived. Again.'

Bo had slunk behind the screen and draped himself against the wall.

'What was all that about?' Brenna asked abruptly. The woman's blows still stung her cheeks. 'What are they accusing me of now?'

Bo smirked, but his brows were hard and humourless. 'It's the same old thing, Brenna. Your blood is cursed, you know. Even the feywalkers want to put an end to it. That you survived last night is almost impressive.'

'Feywalkers?' Brenna repeated. 'What?'

'You know what they say about white wolves.'

Brenna's eyes widened in understanding. She snorted. 'It was just a wolf, Bo. Flesh and teeth. It found its way into Sjavaba – it's as easy as anything to breach the walls – and I was the first person it came across. It wasn't some fey creature exacting punishment on my father's blood, and you'd have to be an idiot to believe that.'

Bo shrugged. 'That's what they're saying.'

'Then they're idiots. But what were they all in here for?'

'Protective charms. Since you didn't die, they say the feywalkers will return, and don't want to be mistaken for their true prey.' He shrugged again. 'But you heard my grandfather. He doesn't go in for those sorts of things.'

Brenna shook her head. 'I can't *believe* this!'

But she could. It was so easy for them to cast blame on her. The keeper's daughter. The one through whom his curse lived on. He'd meddled with things beyond his understanding, beyond his power to control, and it'd been the death of him. That's what they told one another. So of course they believed such a stupid idea, that a wolf was not simply a wolf. That nature itself had condemned her to die for her father's sins.

The front door creaked on its hinges. 'Deal with that, Bo,' Yuel called from the other side of the screen. Bo arched his back and stepped away from the wall, his gaze lingering pointedly on Brenna. She clenched her fists.

'I found this girl half-fainted at the north gate,' a man's voice explained from the other side of the folding screen. 'She wouldn't say what happened to her. We thought it best to bring her to the *apótekari*.'

There was a pause and Brenna assumed Bo was looking over the girl in question. 'My grandfather's dealing with another patient at the moment,' he replied at last. 'But take her to a cot. I'll find something to warm her up.'

Brenna lifted her head to see the newcomer, curious despite her anger. It was unusual for outsiders to visit Sjavaba these days.

The floorboards vibrated as a broad-shouldered man came into view around the edge of the screen. His sun-toned skin, foreign accent, and build suggested he might've once been a sailor, but his grey-and-bronze uniform proclaimed that he now worked as a town watchman. His eyes narrowed when he saw Brenna, but he said nothing. A welcome relief. Instead, he drew in a small, wiry girl.

The stranger looked wild. Her creamy hair fell limp to her shoulders, her feet bare and bruised, streaked with dirt and thin cuts. She was naked but for a thick white pelt that hung from her shoulders down to her knees. Her whole body was rigid, as taut as the skin stretched over her bony frame. Her eyes were huge in her pinched face, pupils almost swallowing the violet of her irises.

She blinked, nose twitching. Her focus snapped to Brenna. Something flickered in her face. Recognition?

Brenna stared at her blankly. She'd never seen the girl before, so why were tears welling in those purple eyes? Why was she stepping away? A stranger to Sjavaba couldn't possibly have heard the townspeople's vile lies about Brenna.

The girl scrabbled at the neck of the pelt, as if it were scorching her. The watchman eyed her with concern.

'*Apótekari!* I think you better come…'

The girl screamed in frustration as her flailing hands failed to haul the pelt from her skin. The watchman jumped. Brenna stared, bewildered. What the hell was wrong with her?

'Bo!'

'Sorry, *Afi.* I don't know what's—'

'She's feverish!' the watchman exclaimed. But he didn't move to help her.

Brenna lurched off the cot, screwing her face up against the pain that flared in her leg. She grabbed the girl's wrists, stilling their frantic movements.

'Hey, hey. Stop it now. You're all right—'

The girl recoiled. She fixed Brenna with wild, anguished eyes, even as she tried to pull away.

'I'm sorry,' she said, her voice a hoarse whisper. 'I'm so sorry.'

'What—'

The girl twisted out of Brenna's grasp and ducked under the watchman's arm. He lunged for her, but she was too quick. Bo darted back into view, blankets spilling out of his arms as he made a belated grab after her. Brenna flung herself forward, crashing into the screen. It gave way under the impact and collapsed with a resounding bang. Brenna fell with it, crying out in pain. She lifted her head just in time to see the girl wrench the door open and leap outside.

'For heaven's *sake*, Bo!'

5

FIADH'S feet slipped on the snow-dusted cobbles as she sprinted into the darker depths of the town, the watchman's boots thundering after her. She darted down a winding alley and edged out the other side. Her lungs were already tight, her breathing shallow and rapid.

If she were found, she'd be dragged back to that eerie room that stunk of herbs, smoke and bloody linen. To the girl with red hair. Fiadh had recognised her at once. The latest victim to the wolf's teeth and claws. Even in her own skin, Fiadh remembered the smell of her blood. Had she not woken with her hands drenched in it? Had she not *tasted* it — the metallic ambrosia the wolf thirsted for, dripping from her own teeth?

The wolf, stirring in the pit of Fiadh's belly, had recognised her too.

Fiadh's stomach churned. She stopped, catching herself on a streetlamp's frozen pole, and vomited. Bile spattered the cobbles. Moaning, she passed a trembling hand over her mouth.

She raised her head. She could hear the watchman's voice, his heavy footfalls. Could smell his sweat and the lingering herbs of the apothecary's shop. If he found her in this state, she wouldn't be able to outrun him.

Fiadh set her jaw and hauled herself to her feet. She wouldn't be caught. Wouldn't be forced back into the same room as her victim. Wouldn't allow herself to be trapped in this town at nightfall, its people innocent to the threat she posed.

Hesitating, she touched the pelt. That was how this had all started in the first place. And the wolf didn't sleep so deeply these days. Should she…

She set her shoulders. While the sun still shone overhead, she would be in control. It would be just for a minute, just to get out.

Fiadh closed her eyes. She wrestled her breathing to a slow and measured rhythm, the musk of the wolf pelt strong in her nose. A shiver ran over her arms, spine, legs. The pelt stung and prickled. Long white fur bristled over her skin, creeping down the length of her arms and legs. Her hair ran down her face, her neck, her collar. She gritted her teeth as her face lengthened, a snarl escaping her widening maw. Her shoulders hunched and she fell forward.

Fiadh shook her body, adjusting to the wolf's shape. She tossed a look over her shoulder, as the watchman blundered into sight, reduced to shades of grey. She jumped and bolted forward, skimming through the streets, swerving expertly in and out of winding back lanes.

The cobbles rippled to rubble beneath her paws. The buildings before her collapsed. Crumbled walls and fallen beams blocked the streets, stinking of mould, refuse, and human waste. But laced through it all, Fiadh could smell the sea.

Soon, her paws clattered on a rotting boardwalk. The town was behind her. Before her, the ocean stretched away to the crisp line of the horizon. She bounded down from the boards to the black sands. The retreating tide hissed and foamed.

Fiadh cocked her ears. All sounds of pursuit had long since faded. But she needed to get out of sight of the town.

She willed herself free of the wolf's body, shuddering as the fur retreated and the frigid coastal wind struck her bare skin. If only she could tear off the rest of the pelt so easily. There had been a time when the wolf's hide had slipped effortlessly from her body. A time when she'd used it with strict caution.

The wolf's strength sapped from her body. Laboured breathing racked her fragile form, rasping in her red-raw throat. She gulped, her mouth dry.

Change back.

Fiadh screwed her eyes shut against the insidious voice. *No*, she protested fiercely. The longer she wore the wolf's body, the more it clung to her. It was only because the sun hung in the sky that she had any control over it at all.

The wolf is stronger than you. It will protect you.

At what cost? Fiadh demanded of herself. The memory of the girl's haggard face and bloodstained clothing flared hideously in her mind. *No! I don't need this wretched pelt!*

Did you not just now rely on its power?

Fiadh bit her lip until blood beaded under her teeth. Anything to shut out the doubts that niggled in the recesses of her mind.

She picked herself up from the sand. It clung to her arms and legs, glittering like stardust on her skin, as she cast her eyes up and down the beach. Where should she go? Where would she be safe? Or rather, where should she hide so the town and its helpless people would be safe from *her*?

The coast stretched far to the west until it reached a wooded headland. But to the east…

Fiadh craned her neck back. As she'd noted from halfway down the lighthouse hill, the town had been built into the crook of the valley. High above her, the tip of the lighthouse's beacon tower could just be seen, bright with a thousand tiny shards of reflected sunlight. The hill beneath it fell to the ocean in a sheer cliff, an outcrop of jagged grey rocks at its base. The tide drew back from them, as if the coast were baring its teeth.

Fiadh stumbled across the sand, making for the outcrop. She touched the cliff's face, surprised at how smooth it was under her hand, and edged around it. The tide lapped at the rocks. She stepped gingerly into the foam. The cuts on her feet stung, but she merely grimaced, squeezing between the outcrop and the base of the cliff. She glanced up and noted the high tide mark above her head. She was only able to come this way because the tide was so far out.

On the other side, Fiadh found the ocean had carved archways in the basalt of the cliff. They gaped dark and hollow, but through the dimness, faint light glowed. They were caves or tunnels, then, through which she might find a beach, blocked from view of the town. From there, she would find a way back to the hills.

And then what?

Survive, she retorted, and set her shoulders.

Her feet pressed neat prints into the sand, marring the delicately shaped ripples crafted by the retreating tide. She edged forward under the shade of the rock, glancing warily over her shoulder as the dark draped over her.

Courtesy of the wolf, her eyes adjusted well to the dimness. The tunnel buckled and curved, the steady work of ocean tides. The low thunder of the ocean rumbled in the cavern, an irregular *drip-drip-drip* echoing within, the walls glistening faintly with water.

A sickening weight coiled in Fiadh's chest, a shuddering fear. She looked over her shoulder again, imagining the tide rushing back to flood the cavern, the waves crashing and beating against the outcrop. Roiling around those jagged teeth to wash into the gaping cave mouth. Swelling and breaking against the walls.

But the wavelets still lapped peacefully at her feet. She licked her bleeding lip and turned back to the cavern. She would be quick. Though she knew very little of the tide or how quickly it might turn, she knew she didn't want to be trapped in this cave when it did.

She shuffled forward and noticed that the ground beneath her feet was dry. At first, she couldn't place why that was important, but after a moment she realised the significance. If the sand had dried since the tide went out, why was the rock still wet?

Fiadh strode quickly to the wall. She ran her hand over the dampness, noting the pattern of algae. Her parched throat urged her to hurry.

There!

A seam of water trickled in fine rivulets down the rock.

She stretched up on her toes and pressed her cupped hands to the wall. Bringing the precious, clouded water to her mouth, she drank thirstily. Her throat begged for more, but she fought back the impulse. This would have to be enough for now. When she got back to the hills she would find cleaner water. Drink snowmelt, perhaps.

Fiadh wiped her mouth. Touching the wall, she continued into the cave. The light faded behind her and she kept her eyes fixed on the faint glow ahead, where the tunnel must end.

When she'd passed halfway through, Fiadh noticed a shift in the wind that whistled through the cavern. With the shift, she caught a welcome scent. She followed it to a shallow, naturally formed basin. A fish, brown and white and as long as Fiadh's forearm, splashed restlessly in its prison.

Fiadh's tongue passed over her chapped lips. She crouched at the edge of the basin, waited with hands poised, then snatched the fish up. It squirmed in her grasp and she dropped it on the bare rock floor. It flopped helplessly, mouth gaping, blank eyes staring. She picked it up again, tightening her grip against its desperate writhing, and bit it just below the head.

Her teeth sank into its flesh. It wriggled. She bit harder, tearing the pink meat. Blood spilled around the corners of her mouth and down her throat. She ripped a strip of its flesh from its fine bones, bolting it down without chewing. The fish's mad writhing ceased and it relaxed, lifeless in her hands.

It disgusted her. As if she were looking at herself from outside her body, watching a taut-skinned girl gorge herself on a raw carcass, smattering blood on the stones at her feet and smearing it on her cheeks, gore dripping down her blue-tinged fingers, down the strands of her tangled hair. Eating like a wolf. It was grotesque.

And it was wonderful.

The soft flesh, salty and sharp on her tongue. The still-warm trickle of blood down her dry throat. A person, a *real* person, couldn't actually like such a meal. Yet, with the wolf pelt clinging tight to her own skin – why, she could enjoy this. Relish it.

Fiadh licked the bones clean and tossed them aside. She leaned forward to wash her hands and face in the rock basin. The water darkened with the fish's blood. Quickly, she stood and crossed the last stretch of the tunnel, as if she could outrun her revulsion.

The opening at the end of the tunnel was much smaller than the entrance – a narrow crevice in the rock, rather than a gaping archway. Grey light filtered weakly through it, along with a muted rushing sound. Fiadh braced her hands on either side of the crevice and poked her head out.

The morning snow had melted into a heavy, wind-driven rainfall. She drew back quickly. Wrung her hands, bit her lip.

'Ouch!'

She brushed a fingertip over the swollen cut. Pressed her palm against her mouth. Tried to calm her mounting fear as the rain poured down outside.

She couldn't go out into that storm. If she got caught with nowhere to warm herself, no way to make a fire, she'd freeze to death. The lighthouse flashed in her mind, but she quashed the idea. Not even a warm hearth could entice her back to that cursed place.

But here…

Fiadh imagined the frothing high tide rushing in on her, with force enough to shatter her against the rocky walls.

She was trapped.

6

BRENNA heard the rain drumming on the roof and groaned inwardly. She wanted to get out of Yuel's shop, back to her hovel, away from Bo's sidelong glances laden with meaning. But there was no way the old apothecary would let her go out into a storm.

When Yuel had finished stitching and dressing her wounds, he'd ordered her to get some sleep and left her alone behind the screen. Only a couple of customers had come to the shop after he'd herded out the crowd of would-be charm buyers, but it was unlikely he'd have more business while the rain poured heavily outside.

Brenna heard Yuel's pensive sigh, the soft shuffle of feet, then the door behind the counter scraping open and clicking shut. It led up to his and Bo's apartments. She remembered a time when a much younger, much friendlier Bo had welcomed her into the private rooms to show her little treasures his parents had brought from a distant corner of the world.

After a moment, the Bo who detested her stepped past the screen, arms crossed.

'I'd be thankful for the rain, you know.'

'What's that supposed to mean?' she snapped.

'Don't be slow,' Bo replied, with equal impatience. 'Those people were going to finish the feywalker's work for it, if you understand me. But they won't come back in this storm. So you should be thankful for it – especially after what the watchman saw.'

Brenna frowned. 'What?'

31

'Ah, yes. *Afi* was fixing you up when the watchman came back, so I don't suppose you heard what he said.'

'Did he find the girl?'

'No. He saw your wolf.'

The hairs on the nape of Brenna's neck prickled. She touched the bandages under her trouser leg. Once more, she was in a twilit street, struggling between the wolf's terrible teeth.

'Where?' she asked. 'Near here?'

'A street away.' Bo peered at her through his lashes. 'And you know what they'll say about that, if you're brighter than you make out.'

'Don't be ridiculous!' Brenna felt the old anger rising like bile in her throat, driving out her fear. 'It's just a wolf. The watchman should've struck it down before it has a chance to hurt anyone else.'

Bo snorted. 'You can't kill a feywalker.'

She wanted to take the crutch Yuel had lent her and whack the smug look off his face. 'Do you believe what they're spouting too, Bo? Use your damned head! In fact, you could all afford to stop and *think!* It's not my fault a rogue wolf is loose in Sjavaba. If the Council had restored the south walls and the harbour district, it wouldn't have been able to get in.'

Bo opened his mouth, but she barrelled on.

'And even if your superstitious charm-buyers are right, feywalkers are spirits of the land. Why would they care about tide curses? Why come now and not years ago? Believe me, I would rather it had killed me that day, before I knew how much hatred a human soul can bear!'

The air rang with the ferocity of her voice.

'Who can know the way of these things?' Bo murmured at last, venom in every syllable. 'Except your father.'

And that, of course, was the crux of it.

The door behind the counter swung open and Yuel hobbled back into the shop. He rounded the screen, a fierce expression weighing on his brows.

'Please,' he said, in a hushed but severe tone. 'I will not put up with all th-this *noise* in my shop!'

'Sorry, *apótekari*,' Brenna said sharply. Swinging her legs over the side of the cot, she propped the crutch under her right arm and eased her weight onto her good leg. She pushed past Bo with as much dignity as she could, though she struggled to manoeuvre the crutch with any level of grace. 'I'll be going.'

Ignoring Yuel's objections, she wrenched the door open and stepped onto the landing, out into the downpour.

⌘

The house was freezing. Brenna could see her breath misting in the air. She shoved the heavy door bolt into place and slumped against the wall, out of breath and soaked through, her hands numb. The walk from the medicine house had been slow and laboured. She'd lost her footing on patchy cobbles, fallen in mud and filth. Her bite wounds flared hot in her cold skin.

Worst of all were the tears stinging her eyes, spilling over her lashes. She sniffed and swiped at her cheeks. So what if they all thought she was cursed? So what if Bo chose to believe them?

Tearing off her dripping coat, she flung it onto the table, atop the bloody rags.

'When winter ends,' she muttered.

She moved to the wide fireplace, where a box of matches sat on the mantelpiece. Snatched it up and lowered herself to the floor, throwing a splintered log from the wood stack into the hearth. Blinked back the tears still beading in her eyes. Shoved kindling into place. Fumbled with the matchbox. Snapped a matchstick in her efforts to light it. Struck another. Held it to the kindling.

'When the new grass grows, buy a busted cart. Buy an old horse bound for the knacker's yard. Ride it through the forests and mountains to the north.'

A delicate yellow flame began licking up the tinder, growing bigger, hotter. Brenna tossed the match into the blaze.

So what if they concocted another reason to hate her? It didn't change anything, really.

She kicked off her boots. Stripped off her clothes, crawled to her bed and hauled the blankets off it. Made a nest for herself under the table before the snapping, crackling fire. The flames, hot and angry and bright, were her sisters. Their leaping tongues spoke to the fire in her chest.

But it *did* matter, she realised with a start. The wolf changed *everything*. Who would sell a cart or horse to a girl they believed cursed, marked for death? Who would defy the wishes of such dangerous spirits, no matter how absurd the idea? They might've been glad to see her leave before this, but now… they would rather kill her with their own hands than let her go.

The old story telling itself anew.

She didn't fight the tears. They smarted on her cheeks. The fire snapped, too hot. She was too close to it, but she didn't move away. Its heat burned the fear clinging to her skin. The heady smell of the wood smoke filled her nose and she breathed it in, welcoming the fire into her lungs. A creeping certainty slowed her racing heart.

There was only one thing she could do. It wasn't simple. It wouldn't be easy. But if she wanted to leave Sjavaba alive, she would have to prove the beast was just that.

She had to kill the wolf.

7

THE tide came in.

Fiadh had feared a sudden powerful surge would roar up the tunnel, barrelling towards her until it caught her, overpowered her, tumbled her, broke her. But when the tide rose, it lapped in gently, licking the tunnel walls. The splashing hiss of it echoed in the cave, peaceful murmurings that mingled lovingly with the steady purr of the rain outside.

Fiadh sat on the floor beside the crevice. Stray rain and sea spray pattered on her legs. She watched the storm-tide waves play down the tunnel, like cubs, tumbling and teasing. Harmless. Until they grew. And that was inevitable.

But for the moment, they were still small, still peaceful.

And Fiadh, she realised, was tired.

Oh so very, very tired.

⌘

A haunting note wavered on the wind.

Fiadh blinked her eyes open. She was lying on the rock floor. The tide lapped at her toes, but the rain had stopped.

She sat up, her body stiff and aching from sleeping on the hard surface. Shuffling forward, she peered out of the crevice.

Tame, billowing clouds scudded across the sky, painted with the gold tones of late afternoon. Black sand swept before her in a neat quarter-moon crescent, skirting the base of high basalt cliffs. She

35

slipped through the cleft in the rock and stepped out into the open.

Again, the floating strain of music shivered through the air. A voice. Clear and resonant and deep. Ethereal and foreign, yet somehow familiar.

Fiadh drifted across the sands, enthralled by the melody. Captive to the voice. The sand glittered in the fading light, as if she were walking on the stars, a moon gliding across the night sky.

The song grew clearer. As she listened, more voices joined the first. Latticed together. Entwined. A choir of eerie beauty. She cast about the shore for the source of the music. Breathed in the ocean's brackish scent. The rich perfume of the recent storm. Salt and rain-washed air. And something new.

Movement caught her eye. She turned to face the waves and blinked. Something was emerging from the water. A low-rolling wave broke behind it, splaying around the approaching shape.

A figure. A person?

Once Fiadh had seen the first, she noticed more rising from the water, all along the crescent shore. And as they rose, the music swelled, foreign words harmonising with the thunder of the ocean.

Fiadh thrilled. With fear? Delight? She couldn't say. Only stood frozen in her suspense.

The first figure drew her feet from the foam. Her body was short and smoothly curved. Long hair fell in streaming rivulets over the folds of her hooded garment, speckled brown like her skin.

Fiadh covered her mouth, eyes wide with recognition.

The other figures joined the first, as their voices had followed hers. They were all similar in form, all with long-lashed round eyes, yet unique in the pattern of their skins, of the fur garments they wore — silver hair pooling into black, salt-white stippled with cream, mouse-brown melting into mahogany.

The woman in the lighthouse, Fiadh thought, her breath snagging in her chest. She could imagine that spectre alongside these women, similar as a sister with her long hair and lashes, her silver-and-fawn skin. And their music! Sung in the same language of that vision's lullaby. Why? Was this a vision too?

Fiadh backed away from the singing apparitions. Her shoulder struck the cliff and she spun around, eyes searching its staggered face for clefts and ledges that she could use to climb it. To get away.

The song swelled, then hushed. Fiadh turned slowly, struggling to quell her treacherous curiosity. The water women stood in the hissing foam, facing one another. They linked their hands. Chanted low, swaying in time to a slow beat. Suddenly, the solemn song broke into something faster, more urgent. And then they were dancing. Forming circles. Clapping hands. Churning the sand with their feet. Spiralling, bending, swaying. Weaving in and around one another. Never breaking the song, which bounced and swelled and skipped.

The brackish scent washed over Fiadh with force, swamping her senses. She rubbed her sensitive nose. So it *was* real after all.

She dug her fingers into the rock. She shouldn't be here. Whatever this dance was, whoever these people were—

One of the dancers, covered in white and brown spots, pulled away from her circle.

Fiadh's heart dropped. She'd been seen!

The water woman ran straight up to her. Her dancing circle rippled and followed. They smiled broadly, merrily, faces flushed with excitement and simple joy. Their bodies moved in an echo of the dance even as they drew apart from it.

They rose around Fiadh like a wave, and she was caught in the swell. They crooned to her, caressed her skin. The spotted woman caught Fiadh's cold-bruised hands and drew her across the sand. Clammy fingers tangled in her hair, slid over her arms, fondled the fur of her pelt. Her heart pounded in time to the lively beat. She tried to protest, but they were a relentless tide and her voice was lost in the tumult of the song, deafening in her ears.

The women reformed their circle and returned seamlessly to the flow of the dance. It broke over Fiadh and tumbled her, tossed her about at its whim. The women's black eyes glittered with amusement. Their hands caught hers to steady her, then to spin her again. The slipping sun traced threads of gold in their hair and splashed their merry faces in gossamer light.

Fiadh's feet snagged in the sand and she fell. But the dancers didn't pause to draw her up again, too enraptured in the melody. They raised their voices to a crescendo, raised themselves onto their toes.

And stopped.

The cut in their song was so abrupt the silence rang. As one, the women turned to the sea and sank to their knees. Deeper voices rumbled to the shore, barely discernible from the ocean's low roar. A whisper sighed through the women. 'The grooms!'

'What?' Fiadh gasped, claiming her voice at last.

The spotted woman butted her head against Fiadh's shoulder, making her start. 'The grooms,' she said. 'The men are joining us.'

The women chimed back, a playful call. The groom's voices replied. A melodic conversation in an evocative and unfathomable tongue. The women – brides – around Fiadh giggled and jumped to their feet, pulling her with them, ready for the next phase of the dance. The surf crashed and brought with it a second wave of the strange people. Grooms flooded and roiled around the brides.

The dance had seemed chaotic before, but Fiadh wondered now whether it could be called a dance at all. The grooms broke into the circles and for a moment the song wavered and fluttered, interrupted. One grasped a bride around her waist and swung her around in the air. Her song burbled around a fit of delighted laughter, the words of the song for him alone. Another groom, black-brown all over, came up beside Fiadh. But he wasn't looking at her. He took the spotted dancer by her hands and drew her in a turn that brought them splashing back into the lapping, fizzing foam. Fiadh lost sight of them as the dance recommenced, falling into a steadier pattern. She stumbled back from it to watch.

In the swirling, rippling, joyous mass, Fiadh saw her. The woman of fawn and silver. The woman from the lighthouse. Dancing with the rest, her expression so light and *glad,* Fiadh doubted she could be the same person who'd sat in that desolate chamber, singing a mournful parody of this bridal song.

Fiadh shook her head, pressing her fingers to her throbbing temples. How could she be here, a vision mingling so boldly with reality?

The dancers surged about her again and swept her into the fray. The woman from the lighthouse and her partner spun towards her. Blurred. Vanished. Fiadh blinked—

A water groom caught her by the arm. She gasped, the spell of the vision broken. The groom was mottled with splotches of black and fawn and silver. Damp silver hair flopped over his brow. His liquid eyes rounded further in surprise when he saw the girl in his arms. But he didn't hesitate in the dance, towing her with him through the steps. A slow smile returned to his lips.

'Túathal,' he said.

'Fiadh.' Her name slipped through her lips unbidden, surprising her.

She danced a turn in Túathal's arms, but the writhing tide of bodies tore them apart. A second groom took her hands, then another as the dance continued. Fiadh's vision blurred, her head light. She locked eyes with Túathal across the circle and he grinned. She caught glimpses of the spectral woman, her garment slipping from her shoulders in the excitement of the dance, tender love in her partner's eyes. Túathal's playful smile once more.

Fiadh faltered. Pressed a hand to her spinning head. The dance swirled around her, relentless as storm seas.

The pace of the song slowed, as the dancing rings mingled. Fiadh's circle was sucked back into the mass, leaving her crouched in the sand, like flotsam abandoned by the tide.

The grooms and brides separated, the women drawing together. Fiadh lifted her head to watch. The brides raised their voices and even though Fiadh couldn't understand the language of the words, their question rang clearly. The grooms' resonant voices sung an answer.

The melody hung in the air. Solemn. Joyous.

The water people laughed breathlessly, bodies reeling from the dance. They hugged, kissed each other on foreheads and noses, cheeks or lips.

Now that it was over, Fiadh noticed the light had faded. She looked wildly to the west. Only the faintest glow lingered behind the rocky projection that cut off the crescent beach. When the ocean had swallowed the last of the day… she looked down at her hands, at the wolf's pelt. Then up the basalt cliff.

She became aware that the strange people had started moving away from the churned-up sand where they'd danced, settling at the base of the cliffs. The brown-and-white spotted woman and her partner lay down a little apart from their neighbours. The groom stroked his bride's hair from her brow and kissed her forehead. Groups of friends nuzzled one another and nestled into the star-glitter sand as if it were a vast bed.

Outside the feverish dance, Fiadh shivered, her teeth starting to chatter. She rubbed her hands together. Numb fingers and toes wouldn't do – she needed to climb out of here. She'd fled the town hoping to be far from people by the time the wolf crept over her skin and shadowed her mind.

'Fiadh?'

She started and twisted around. Túathal stood above her, the silver of his skin and coat glowing against the gathering dark.

'What are you?' she whispered, the words an unplanned sigh. She blinked. Shook her head to clear it. That didn't matter. She didn't want to know. Of all the world's bounteous mysteries, she already had one too many to unravel.

But Túathal lowered himself to sit next to her. Leaned forward, his breath warm in her ear.

'Selkies,' he whispered.

She jumped, staring at him. Struggled to her feet and spun around to look at the others. Blinked, rubbed her eyes. In the place where the water dancers had sunk to rest as forgeries of humankind, seals clustered. Snuffing through their noses. Making high crooning calls to one another. Rubbing their heads over each other's necks and bodies as they settled.

'Skin changers,' Túathal added, rising to stand beside her. 'As are you.' She faced him. He grinned, open and playful. As if the concept was amusing, beautiful. Rather than abhorrent.

Fiadh crossed her arms over the pelt that coated her torso. She shook her head fiercely.

'No,' she gasped. 'No. No, no, *no!*'

She backed away from him, from *them*. Spun around and ran to the jagged cliff. Leapt onto the nearest ledge. Jarred her knee on the rock. Sucked in a sharp breath, but pressed on, shambling up the basalt columns. Her arms prickled warningly. The pelt dragged heavily on her skin.

'Fiadh!'

She hesitated, fighting the pull to look over her shoulder, to look down. But for a third time, Túathal's words incited an unwilling response. She looked back.

The spotted dancer was sitting up among the seals, her hands hovering at the hem of her glossy hood. Brown and salt-white hair fell back from her upturned, pouting face. There was a shuffle of motion and more of the selkies' hoods slid away to show their near-human faces, all turned to the girl clinging to the cliff.

At a distance from the rest, Túathal stood watching her, though she couldn't make out his expression.

'Will you return, Fiadh?' he called. Simply curious.

A tremor quavered over her body. She gasped and clawed her fingers in the rock. The wolf was waking.

'Yes.'

A final, involuntary reply.

⌘

The lighthouse's weathered door shrieked across the slate.

Fiadh slammed it shut. Ran her hands blindly over the doorjamb, searching for some sort of bolt or lock – *there!* The cold metal stung her fingers, which already bristled with fur. She shoved the latch down into place, locking herself in the lighthouse. Another tremor racked through her, ripping a scream from her throat. She thrust herself away from the door and flung her arms out imploringly.

'What do you want?' she cried into the darkness. 'Why are you showing her to me?'

Her head throbbed. Her jaw ached and prickled. She bared her teeth, trying to fight it.

Fight back!

She sank to the floor. Curled her legs against her chest. Wrapped her arms tight around them, nails biting into her skin as spasms shook her. Felt her body shift under her palms. The change was fast when she surrendered to it, as she often did, too tired to fight it. But if she never fought it, would she lose herself completely? Until the wolf was all that was left?

She pressed her face to her knees and wailed, screamed, cursed. Tears streamed down her cheeks and across the bridge of her nose, pooling in her hair. She would never be able to return to her father like this. Even if, by some miracle, she found him again. It would break his heart.

Fiadh moaned, long and low.

'Why?' Her voice was thin and weak, muffled by the pelt. She was so small in the room, the weight of the night pressing in on her. 'You sing a song, you show me some woman. What's it for? What do you want me to do? Don't you see me? I can't—'

Her eyes flew open. She bolted upright.

The woman!

A strong wind blew through the lighthouse, keening in the roof and beacon tower. The structure groaned. Fiadh stared up into the rafters, heart hammering in the cage of her chest.

'The woman.' Fiadh licked her lips. 'She was like me? Those people are her people. So she was a selkie – a skin changer – too?'

She remembered the first vision. Saw it vividly. The woman of fawn and silver had worn a pelt garment on the beach. But in the lighthouse, she'd worn a shift, a human dress. Between these walls, she'd been free of her other skin.

'Fine. If you're offering answers rather than questions, show me all the visions you want! Show me how to break this curse!'

The lighthouse settled. The keening wind died down.

An accord had been struck.

8

BRENNA woke to a barrage of knocking on her hovel's heavy door. She jerked up and cracked her head on the underside of her table. Cursing, she untangled herself from the nest of bedding and groped for her crutch.

'This is the Sjavaba Watch!' His shout rattled the door almost as much as his fist had. 'Keeper's daughter! Come out!'

'If you wait a bloody second, I will!' she shouted back. Shuffling out from under the table, she clutched at it with one hand, pushing off the ground with the crutch under her other arm. Pain flared hot along the stitched-together seams of her bite wounds, lancing behind her eyes. She clenched her jaw to stop herself from crying out.

The watchman hammered the door again. Brenna limped around the table, shoved the bolt away and opened the door. He was a barrel-chested man with hammy fists, his bulk mostly obscuring the cohort standing ready behind him. As he looked down his bulbous nose at her, she caught a whiff of something like heather. A tiny cloth pouch was tied around his throat.

He was wearing a charm – for protection, against her! She almost snorted. In her current state, he could knock her over with his pinkie.

The hint of his fear made her bold. She squared her shoulders and stood as straight as she could. 'What's this about?'

'The Council summons you.'

'Oh, good. I thought it might've been something important.' Brenna pulled her lips back from her teeth in a snarl that might pass for a smile. 'Well, if it's all the same to the Council, I have other plans for today.'

'It's a *summons*, not a request,' the captain growled.

'What's it about?' Brenna asked, feigning ignorance. She caught a flicker of movement from the cohort behind him but forced her eyes to maintain contact with his.

'Don't play the fool. It concerns the wolf.'

'How kind of them to ask how I'm recovering from my ordeal. Actually, my wounds are a bloody pain and I can't possibly manage the walk to the Council chambers. But if those sweethearts want to know how they can assist me, they could start with rebuilding the southern walls—'

'Enough of your insolence, curse bearer!' the watchman roared. He grabbed her by her shoulder, yanking her out into the street. The rough movement agitated her injury and she cried out despite her best efforts.

She opened her mouth, ready to assault him with a torrent of foul language, but clamped it shut again. The least that would earn her was a cuff to her already throbbing head. If the Council wanted to see her, they would. But it would be on her terms.

She thrust up her chin. 'Fine.'

The watchman nodded, satisfied, and looked over his shoulder. 'Kasim. Ruo.'

Two of the bronze-trimmed cohort — the broad-shouldered watchman Brenna recognised from the medicine house and a man with Bo's silky black hair – stepped forward. Kasim took the lead, Ruo falling in behind her. Their captain barked an order and the rest filed after them.

Brenna kept her eyes forward, fixed on Kasim's broad back. She focused on wielding her crutch and walking as smoothly as she could over the iced cobbles. It was imperative that she looked in control. Not cowed or worried. Not broken.

She arranged her features into a mask, but behind her set jaw and fixed eyes, her mind whirred. In the scorching heat of her kitchen fire, she'd thought she would carry out her plan furtively. She'd imagined striding into the town square, dragging the wolf's bloodied carcass over the uneven cobbles, relishing in the townspeople's scandalised expressions when she deposited it in the middle of the square.

But this was still possible even if the Council knew of her goal. In fact, she thought, as the watchmen guided her across the square and towards the Council chambers, she could use this.

The heavy-set captain held out his arm and Ruo gripped Brenna's shoulder to stop her. She grunted, jerking her arm free, but waited as the captain ascended the chamber's broad stone steps. When Sjavaba's central hub had been closer to the docks, the building had been a private home owned by one of the Old Families, from which the Council members were drawn. It had been converted promptly after the devastation of the southern district.

The captain conferred with the two guards manning the doors. They looked down the steps to where Brenna waited. She held her head high and met their eyes. At a signal from his captain, Kasim waved his hand for Brenna to approach. Before Ruo could shove her from behind, she shuffled forward. Angled her crutch, placed it on the first step, then moved her right leg. Dragged her wounded leg up after her. Repeated the agonisingly slow process until she reached the guards, who opened the doors. Limped into the foyer.

Brenna hadn't been inside these chambers before and let her eyes rove around them. It still felt like a wealthy man's house rather than a public building – the paintings lining the walls were not of councillors of the past or present, instead striking Brenna as an aristocrat's personal collection. Vast seascapes hung high on the wall, framed with gilt. Expressive oils depicted familial faces and poses, unorthodox styles from the days Sjavaba had received foreign merchants and powerful people from across the oceans.

Brenna allowed a sneer to crack her mask. Even here were reminders of the past wealth of Sjavaba. Of times before the ocean became their gaoler, before her father was held responsible for it.

Kasim and Ruo stood with her by the front doors while their captain went ahead. Brenna closed her eyes and took a deep breath, silently rehearsing what she'd say. Her stomach fluttered. What if the Council decided to believe the nonsense about feywalkers? Remembering how they'd dealt with her father, she shuddered.

'They'll see you now.'

Brenna looked up. The captain had returned.

It was time.

She tossed her mass of curls and struck out across the foyer. Ruo led the way through the inner doors and down a short corridor, which was inset with alcoves filled with decorative vases, candle stands, and statuettes, further reminders of Sjavaba's lost pride.

At the end of the corridor, they came into the Council's courtroom.

Brenna paused on the threshold to take it in. It was clear that it'd once been the house's grand dining hall – the ceiling was higher than the foyer's and an ornate fireplace was set into the right-hand wall. The floor was laid with tiles of grey and brown slate, the panelling dark wood, which made the room feel oppressively dim. Shards of washed-out sunlight cut sharply from windows set high on the far wall, striking the tiles like solid silver bars, separating Brenna from the people within. Beyond the pale beams, Brenna could faintly see a long, curved bench. Figures shifted in the gloom, seated at a raised table so they loomed over those who entered their court.

Unbidden, Brenna limped into the centre of the hall and stood before the assembled Council. The stark light made her blink and she instinctively ducked her head. Her hair fell forward. It blazed in the light, alive with tongues of yellow and gold, amber and red, bidding her to be as brazen. She lifted her chin and fixed her eyes on the row of shadowy forms before her.

'I demand the Council's official protection.'

Her voice boomed in the large hall. She couldn't see the

councillors' faces but heard a sharp intake of breath and low mutterings from the dimness. Her breathing quickened with nerves, but she pushed on before they could stop her.

'The people of Sjavaba have spoken a grave accusation against me. Grant me freedom to prove the wolf that attacked me was no more than—'

'Stop!' the captain bellowed. She heard the pounding of feet, moments before Kasim ran into the light and grabbed her roughly. She spun to face him, to shake him off, but he wasn't looking at her. He bowed his head to the obscured councillors.

'Apologies, Elders!' he said. 'We brought her here for your judgement of yesterday's incident, at your request. *Not* to hear this nonsense.'

Brenna wrenched her arm free and staggered back, just managing to keep her footing. 'It's not nonsense!' she protested, appealing directly to the councillors. 'Elders, I'm sure you've heard rumours, though I believe you won't find me guilty on such shallow grounds. *You* are wise, pragmatic people. But the townspeople are easily swayed and quick to judge. I ask for your protection and offer my help to get rid of this wild animal.'

Her words echoed without challenge or assent in the cavernous hall. She gritted her teeth, but the shadowy figures made no sound. Vaguely, she sensed a second watchman move to her side and take her arm, as Kasim tightened his grip. Still, the Council remained silent.

Suddenly, her simmering frustration boiled into outright anger. She twisted out of the watchmen's arms and lunged forward out of the light, throwing herself against the raised table. The sudden contrast blinded her but she stared fiercely into the darkness.

'Say something!' she shouted. 'You're Sjavaba's leaders, aren't you?' She punched the bench. 'Quit hiding in the dark while your town crumbles into ruin!'

Strong, rough hands caught her arms. Her crutch clanged loudly on the tiles as Kasim and Ruo heaved her back from the table. She squirmed in their grip, but only hurt herself. Her movements strained against her stitches and she cried out in pain. She heard movement from the table. Chairs scraping back, people leaping to their feet. A buzz of voices.

'Wait,' a soft voice spoke.

The watchmen stopped short. Brenna struggled to get her feet under her, gingerly taking her own weight. She raised her eyes. With the crisp light from the windows at her back and her vision adjusted to the gloom, she could finally see the Council with some clarity.

Eight men and three women stood behind the table. From the days Sjavaba had seen free mingling with travellers from across the seas, its people were diverse in feature and tongue. But the Council members, drawn from the Old Families, all had fair skin. Their hair had faded in most cases to grey or white. Brenna caught a glimpse of Elder Emil, his dirty blonde hair pulled back in tight braids, his thin-lipped mouth hard. She also recognised Eldress Aoife and Elder Johan. The red had faded from their heads, but Brenna knew them to be her distant relatives.

The twelfth councillor, the one who'd spoken, was rising slowly to his feet. The others quieted. Eldress Aoife held out her arm to support him. He swept a stray strand of thin white hair off his brow and lowered his milky eyes to look at Brenna.

High Elder Fólki rested his hands on the tabletop and leaned forward. The chief councilman waited until his fellow members settled. After everyone else had resumed their seats, Emil remained standing. He exchanged a charged look with Fólki, but finally sat down, his piercing eyes turned to Brenna. She ignored him and set her face towards the High Elder.

'For clarity, daughter of the fallen keeper, what is the charge brought against you?' Although his voice was barely louder than a whisper, it rang clearly in the silent room.

Brenna shook her head, a bitter smile twitching her lip. 'I won't say it, High Elder Fólki. It isn't true, and you will not hear self-condemning words from *my* mouth.'

Fólki held up his hand to preempt the mutterings of his fellow councillors. 'In that case… Eldress Aoife. Please repeat the charges for which the keeper's daughter has been summoned.'

The woman wore her hair in neat, coiled plaits, not a strand out of place. 'She is the bearer of a curse, councillors, deserving the ire of the fey,' she declared dispassionately. 'A white wolf attacked her two nights ago and returned yesterday to finish its work.'

'We cannot tolerate a curse-bearer among us!'

'Peace, Emil,' Fólki sighed without looking. He gestured to Brenna. 'And you refute this accusation?'

'Yes, High Elder. It was only a wolf that attacked me. Nothing more.'

The courtroom fell silent. Brenna's heart clenched tightly in her chest. Or perhaps it was her lungs. She struggled to keep her breathing even.

After a moment that felt like an hour to Brenna, the High Elder leaned back and cast his pale eyes over the assembled councillors. 'As I see it,' he began slowly, 'I agree with the keeper's daughter. The events before us are not enough to prove the wolf was an agent of natural justice.'

'What of justice and retribution for our families, Fólki?' Elder Emil exclaimed, leaping to his feet. 'My daughters are widows because of that girl's father! And even now, the keeper's curse plagues us, long after his death. The tide drowns any who seek our harbour and any who risk leaving it. Her blood is tainted – we will be safe once she's dead!'

The councillors on either side of him shouted their assent.

High Elder Fólki swayed, as if the effort of announcing his verdict had been too much for him. Eldress Aoife took his arm and helped ease him into his seat.

'I did not say there would be no justice or retribution. The daughter herself has provided the solution.'

Fólki sighed, closing his eyes. The councillors exchanged glances and muttered to one another. Aoife gave him a gentle nudge. Nodding, he rubbed his eyes back open and made an effort to sit straighter in his chair.

'I propose we grant her request for protection,' he said. Elder Emil opened his mouth to argue, but Fólki cut him off. 'One month. For one month, no one will be permitted to harm her. In that time, she will be given freedom to hunt the wolf.' Leaning his elbows on the table, he regarded Brenna. 'If you succeed in killing it, we will accept that this incident wasn't the result of a curse, as feywalkers cannot be destroyed. However, in the case that it is a feywalker, we cannot provide protection and will not intervene.'

Brenna pushed herself away from Ruo and Kasim. 'And when I kill it, you will provide me with a horse and cart so I can leave Sjavaba.'

Elder Emil and several others shouted and rose to their feet. Kasim shook her shoulder and apologised to the Council. But Brenna's eyes were fixed on the High Elder's ancient, withered face.

'Why do you protest?' High Elder Fólki asked, holding Brenna's gaze. 'Either way, we will rid Sjavaba of the keeper's blood.' He gathered himself and stood again. 'Are there any objections?'

Elder Emil threw a dirty look at Brenna, but clearly felt he couldn't argue with the proposition. Brenna held herself rigid, fighting the traitorous tremor in her legs.

'Then as we have spoken, so it will be.'

In unison, the councillors thumped their right palms on the table. The decisive bang resounded heavily in the room. Brenna's legs gave way and she sank to the floor, letting her breath go in a sigh of relief.

9

FIADH lowered herself down the surface of the rock. Her heart thumped almost painfully in her chest, but not in fear that she would slip from the considerable height, though her body was weak from her sleepless night.

Excitement quickened her pulse. A thrumming anticipation that she might find answers to the curse of the wolf pelt, a way to free herself from its strengthening hold on her.

She jumped down the last couple of feet onto the sand and swept her hair away from her face. The crescent beach arced out to her left and right, framing the choppy grey-blue waters. She cast her gaze down its smooth curve. It was empty. She ran to where the selkies had nested to sleep the night before, but there was no sign of them. Even the furrows they'd dug with their wild dancing had been washed away by the night's high tide. The beach looked as deserted as it had before the first brides had risen from the waves.

Her excitement juddering into unease, Fiadh ran to the lapping water and scanned the surf urgently with her eyes. 'Túathal!' she called. She cupped her hands around her mouth. '*Túathal!* I need to talk to you!'

The ragged wind beat against her face, buffeting her eyelashes. She ran her hands through her hair, clasping them at the base of her neck so the creamy strands wouldn't obscure her sight. Still, she saw nothing but the waves, heard nothing but their persistent thunder. She glanced up towards the lighthouse, just visible over the western ridge of the cliffs, but no answer rested with its brooding shadow. Dragging her eyes back to the waves, she forced herself to take a deep breath. She sat in the sand and wrapped her arms around her knees.

She waited an hour on the beach. The foam crept up to her toes, as a fleecy blanket of light grey cloud blew over the sky. A fine misting rain began to fall and Fiadh lifted her face heavenward to welcome it.

Her nose wrinkled as she caught a scent she recognised, rolling off the salty surf. She heard the wet crunching of feet on sand.

'Fiadh?'

Túathal stopped in front of her. He was soaked. Water streamed from his hair and down his face, his arms, his fur coat. Dripped from his chin, his fingers. He grinned, teeth flashing white against the fawn patch smeared on his jawline, the corners of his deep black eyes crinkling. He crouched down in front of her. Behind him, she could see more of the selkies rising from the water, pushing back their hoods.

'I was worried you'd left,' Fiadh said. She unfurled her body and rested her legs in the fizzing foam. 'I need to talk to you.'

Túathal cocked his head. 'Then why were you in such a rush last night?'

Fiadh twisted her hands in her lap, unsure of how much to say and how much to hide. But did she even need to hide anything from these people? They were like her. Possessors of two skins. They would understand.

'I… I was really lost last night.' She paused, half expecting Túathal to say something. But he only shifted higher up the sands and settled next to her, his eyes wide and attentive. 'You said you're skin changers. I am too.'

A slow smile spread over Túathal's face. 'I thought so.' He leaned closer and tweaked the edge of the wolf pelt. 'You look like one of us.' He met her eyes and laughed suddenly. 'Except bits of you look too human.'

Fiadh's tongue stuck to the roof of her mouth. He was invasively close. 'That's what I wanted to ask you about,' she said, at last finding her voice. She took a deep breath—

And yelped. A blur of white and brown butted into her and knocked her, sprawling, into the sand. The spotted selkie woman from the night before kissed her cheek, wet hair pouring over Fiadh's face. Túathal gave a bark of laughter, as the bride sat up, grinning. Lightly nudging the other selkie aside, Túathal took Fiadh's hands to pull her upright. She panted, dazed by the woman's sudden appearance.

'Gentler, Dula,' Túathal chided lightly, as if he were speaking with a rambunctious child. His hands still held Fiadh's. 'She was talking to me—'

'What's your name?' Dula interrupted. 'Where did you go last night? You could have slept with us!' She cupped Fiadh's cheeks with clammy hands and exclaimed, 'Your eyes! They're the colour of the dusk-time sky!' Her fingers trailed to tangle in Fiadh's hair, looping strands around them, her eyes alight with fascination. 'You're kind of pretty, for a human.'

Fiadh's breath snagged in her throat. Dula's excitement was stifling.

'Dula, she's a skin changer.'

She chirped with delight. Flinging her arms around Fiadh, Dula kissed her cheek again. Yanked Fiadh's hands from Túathal's and danced to her feet, hauling Fiadh after her with surprising strength. 'Swim with me!'

Fiadh opened her mouth to protest, but Dula had already dragged her ankle-deep into the water. Several more selkies pooled around her, crooning and chirruping, sounds more suited to their animal skin. Túathal splashed into the shallows with them.

'Swim with us,' they sang, as they drew her further into the water.

'I can't!' Fiadh argued, trying to break away.

But it *can.*

The waves splashed her chest, as the selkies drew their hoods over their heads and ducked under the surface. Fiadh covered her mouth.

Seals bobbed in the water around her, speckled and spotted and patched, liquid eyes glittering with mirth. Whiskers sprouted around their noses, tickling her bare arms. A silver seal with black and fawn patches brushed around her, spinning her on the spot. Her toes lost touch with the sand. The frigid water had sapped the feeling from her limbs and she floundered, spluttering as brackish water swamped her nose and mouth.

They'll drown me!

The wolf is strong. It will save you.

She gave in.

The wolf pelt prickled savagely, consuming her. The selkies chirped in alarm and pulsed away. The wolf's body was strong. Fiadh kicked her legs and paddled around them, her muzzle skimming easily above the water. The selkies swam closer to sniff her. She felt whiskered noses nudging her flanks. A spotted seal, which Fiadh recognised as Dula, threw back her head and let out a braying laugh.

Laughter escaped from Fiadh's panting mouth too, a whining bark. The selkies seethed around her. One after the other, they ducked under the waves. She felt their movement stir the water beneath her feet. Hesitating only a second longer, she dipped her head below the surface and kicked out after them. The selkies were sleek shadows in the green-grey depths. She kept pace with them for a way, skimming just under the skin of the sea. Like the images carved on the chest in the lighthouse chamber, the selkies tumbled and played with one another, coiling and twining along each other's bodies. And Fiadh saw that it was another dance.

She swam down to meet them. Dula butted her nose, as Túathal spiralled under her belly. The others tumbled around her. A warm, tainted emotion blossomed in Fiadh's chest. She nuzzled the selkies and then disengaged from their dance, striking up towards the surface, breaking into the open air.

'Are you tired?'

Túathal bobbed in the water beside her, the hood of his selkie skin slipping onto his shoulders.

Giving no answer, Fiadh paddled away from him and swam for the beach. When her paws scraped the boggy sands, she forced the wolf back. It snagged at the corners of her mind, but she shook herself free and crawled onto the shore, trembling with cold. She sat above the lap of the tide and hugged herself to quiet the shivers wracking her frail human frame.

'Fiadh, what's wrong?'

Túathal sat next to her. She raised her head to look at him properly. He had a round, open face, a mouth ready to laugh. But he wore a concerned expression, the sort that made her feel they'd known each other a long time. She turned her face to the sea, to the greys and blues and greens of the winter horizon. Now that the time had come, her body felt suddenly stiff and jittery. She'd kept her story a secret so long her body fought against her spilling it.

'Túathal, have you ever met a feywalker? They're skin changers like you.'

The selkie man cocked his head. A slow grin warmed his face. 'Yes. If that's what you are, then yes. I have now.'

Fiadh bowed her head. 'I am not a feywalker. I'm not meant to be a skin changer. You and your people… your pelts belong to you. But I was born with one skin.' She glanced at Túathal to check if he was following. His expression hadn't changed, so she powered on. 'The pelt I wear was stolen from one years ago and given to me.' She tucked her arms against the coarse fur, a wry twist curling her lip. 'To keep me safe.'

Túathal thrust himself closer, clutching Fiadh's arm. She started. His face was alight with interest. 'How?'

'Like… yours?'

Túathal frowned and looked down at his own patchy pelt. 'It doesn't protect me.'

'Yes, it does. A human couldn't survive in the ocean as you do, or swim so long in water so cold. Pelts give you strength we don't share.

That's what my father wanted – for me to use the pelt to survive. So I could run faster and hunt for my food. So I could smell danger and slip away. So I would stay alive long enough to find him again. But…' She broke off in a sob.

Túathal's hands were suddenly on her cheeks, his brow furrowed in concern. She flinched. His face was too close. Pulling away from him, she thrust his hands away.

'Don't,' she pleaded, swiping at her weeping eyes. 'Please. Don't get so close.'

Even as she said it, she wished she could welcome his touch, his curious nearness. But she couldn't, any more than she could take part in his people's play, their dances and caresses. So familial, as if they knew her.

But if they knew her, they would be afraid.

'I'm sorry.'

Fiadh lurched to the surface of her turbulent mind and looked up at Túathal. He held his hands close to his body, his face turned away from her. He clearly didn't understand why she'd refused his touch. Her explanation had only baffled him more. It was clear that these people – these strange form-shifters resting in the sands and playing in the frigid winter seas – were affectionate with one another, open and honest and spirited. Fiadh was foreign to them. Her confusion and turmoil, her paradox of desires.

Out of place. She was always out of place.

She reached out, hesitated, and touched his hand. Feather-light and tentative. He turned to her and she drew back.

'I'm not angry.' She tried to smile. 'I'm confused. And lost. Your people… I've never met anyone like you before. Please. I want to learn more about you so I can understand *this*' – she pressed a hand to the fur covering her chest – 'better. So I can control it.'

So it doesn't control me.

Not to cast it aside?

Fiadh squirmed at the snide thought. She pushed it away.

'Control it?' Túathal echoed.

She nodded. 'When my father first gave me the pelt, he told me it was stronger than me, that I could become stronger with it. But he warned me to use it sparingly, only when I felt most threatened. And for a while, I was very careful. I didn't even try it for a long time. But when I did…'

Sighing, she closed her eyes, remembering that long-ago day. The thrill of fear at discovering she was being pursued, whether by thieves or creditors, she hadn't guessed. Her heart-pounding flight. The moment when, cornered as hunted prey, she'd realised she would have to use her father's gift. Frantic moments stripping her clothes off so she could enfold herself in the pelt's coarse fur. Its heady musk filling her nostrils.

The first time the wolf had woken to her had been exhilarating. It had banished her fear and stolen her away.

'I was strong. I was bold. It was everything I wanted to be,' she said.

Túathal laughed. An outburst of joyful appreciation. 'Yes!' he exclaimed. He leapt to his feet, grinning. 'We are the same! Our two skins give us such freedom – I see whales and they're bigger than us, more powerful, but I laugh at them because although they leap in the air, they know nothing of it. We step out in these forms and can bask in the sun and dance!' He gestured and moved his body with excitement, with pure vibrancy. 'We sing with voices no whale nor shark nor common seal could ever comprehend! And we see humans from afar, on their vessels, afraid of the water – of its might and its depth – and I laugh at them too. They cannot race in the tide as we do!'

Fiadh's lips trembled, as something became clear as fine glass.

'We're not the same,' she said, regret heavy in her words.

Túathal's grin weakened and he lowered his arms. 'Why not?'

'My skin was stolen. It wasn't meant for me, and I'm paying the price. The wolf won't let me go anymore. I've relied on it too much.

It's growing stronger and eventually, it won't need me. I've been… its vessel. But soon it will be able to go alone, and I…' Her words stuck in her throat. She swallowed, pushing herself to speak what she'd known for the past season. 'I will be lost.'

Fiadh gathered herself and rose from the glitter-black sand.

She swept her eyes up the shore. For a moment, she paused to appreciate the simple happiness she could see, could hear.

But could not be a part of.

The selkies resting between the cliffs and tide had formed a loose circle, singing. Not as before. Not wild and passionate, nor haunting and mysterious. It was loving and sweet, gentle and warm. Charming and clumsy, broken often by comfortable laughter. Grooms and brides curled up to one another as they sang. Friends played with each other's hair as their voices wove something richly familial.

Fiadh turned and left.

10

NIGHT had fallen, but Túathal still stood in the rising swell of the tide, staring at the basalt cliffs, as if the milk-skinned girl would climb down again at any moment.

He did not join his clanmates in their singing and dancing as they returned to the shore for the night. The familiar suck and swell of the water around his knees were dissonant with Fiadh's words, her anguish. The feelings she expressed had been agitated, complicated. Pained and painful. Utterly foreign.

Túathal knew fear and sorrow and grief. Though he and his clan laughed at the creatures of the sea, they knew the terror of shark teeth and fishers' harpoons, the danger of storms and even their beloved tide. But he'd never feared his own skin.

The moon had risen and illuminated the beach in a pale, pearly light. At the corner of his eye, Túathal noticed a figure approaching him. He recognised Dula's groom by his black-brown skin and garment, which trailed across the sand as he moved with characteristic dignity towards Túathal.

'Quillen,' Túathal said, rousing himself. He stepped forward to greet his friend.

'What are you doing, brother?' Quillen asked, in his resonant baritone voice.

'I'm waiting for her to come back.'

'The girl who appeared for the bridal dance?' Casting his eyes to the cliff face, Quillen arched his eyebrows. 'A curious thing.'

'A skin-changer with a stolen pelt,' Túathal mused. He reached forward and took Quillen's hands, as though the other man were his tether to normality. 'Have you ever heard of such a thing?'

Quillen bowed his head. 'I have heard of stolen skins, brother.'

Involuntarily, Túathal took a step back, the incoming tide rising to his thighs. Quillen drew him up out of the waters and onto the higher, dry sands.

'If she possesses a stolen pelt, Túathal, we must be wary of her.'

'I don't believe she's dangerous.'

Quillen shrugged. 'Perhaps not, but I see no reason to wait for her in the waves alone when we are still celebrating the season.'

Túathal dropped Quillen's hands and smiled, a little forlornly. 'I'm happy for you and Dula, my brother, but I'm out of place among you now.'

'You are no less a part of our clan because you have no bride, Túathal.' The words sounded stern, though Túathal knew he meant them kindly. 'And you aren't the only one this season. Ungi, Halfan, Edda, and others likewise chose no partners, yet they have joined the—'

Túathal grasped Quillen's arm. 'Swim with me!'

Quillen blinked. 'What? Túathal…'

But Túathal had already leapt back into the waves, the water beating against his chest. Spinning, he raised his hands to the hood of his pelt and grinned at his friend. He flipped the hood up and ducked under the moonlit breakers. Below the silver-skinned surface, the ocean's heavy darkness pressed in on him. His form shifted and changed, arms flattening into paddle-like flippers, legs fusing together as the pelt crept down the length of his body, forming a powerful tail. He reopened his eyes, now resting in a long-nosed, whiskered face.

Túathal kicked forward, gliding further and deeper. He heard a muted splash and a moment later Quillen's sleek dark form soared past him. He spiralled playfully around his friend's body, then veered off. Satisfied that Quillen was following at his tail, Túathal guided them where he wanted to go. The pair skimmed close to the undulating surface, the filtered moonlight dancing on their backs.

Túathal led the way east along the coastline of steep cliffs, twining around cruel rocky outcrops, the ocean floor dropping into deep green-black darkness below them. The relentless pounding of the sea over millennia had hollowed caverns and crevices in the rock of the cliffs. Eventually, they dropped away into a delta. A river, flowing from the mountains inland, split in a network of rivulets down the sediment projection, reaching like long, crooked fingers to touch the sea.

Túathal finally turned and guided Quillen towards the shore, between the delta and the depression of the craggy coastline. He could taste the mingling of fresh river and brackish ocean waters, a strange marriage of two worlds.

Quillen tossed back the hood of his seal skin. Wearing his human shape, he prodded Túathal's back with his toe and jerked his head upwards. They both bobbed to the surface. Quillen paused to slick his glossy hair back from his face.

'I imagine the only reason we're out this far is that you want to speak freely,' he said firmly, panting a little. He reached out a hand to Túathal's whiskered face and shoved the hood free. It fell back, trailing on the surface of the water. 'So talk. I'm listening.'

Túathal ducked his head to half-hide in the lapping water. Drifting backwards, he sought the seafloor with his toes. He set his feet on the silty floor and waded back onto the stretch of beach, Quillen following, until they both rested on the sand. Túathal stared at the frayed ribbons of the river coursing over black sediment. His friend watched his face, waiting.

'Quillen,' Túathal began at last. 'How did you… know? With Dula?' He didn't wait for an answer, still gazing into the distance. 'My father said it was like instinct, like knowing where to migrate and when. Like the moon and tide – a clear pull that takes time to understand, but before you know it, you've followed. He said my mother was a dear friend and he admired her spirit. But it was only on his bridal night that he knew he loved her. When the women sang, he found he could hear her voice as if she sang for him alone. And when they danced, he said he had no more questions, because she was the answer to every one.'

Sighing, Túathal ran his hands through his damp curls, resting them at the base of his neck. 'I really wanted answers when we left for our bridal dance, Quillen. But nobody sang to me from the beach. When we all danced, I didn't feel drawn to anyone. No one sought me out.'

Túathal paused, a small smile touching his mouth. He turned to his friend and shrugged. 'Then, I found myself dancing with her.' Reaching out, he gripped Quillen's shoulder. 'I don't know what it is about her. I don't know if this is how you feel about Dula. But I feel like she holds answers.'

'You want the pelt-stealer for your bride?' Quillen asked incredulously.

Túathal shook his head. How could he make his friend understand what he now felt with such conviction? 'No. That wasn't the answer I wanted. That's not the answer I've been seeking. I only now realise that's not the question I've been asking.'

'What *have* you been asking?' Quillen pressed, leaning closer.

'My mother.'

Túathal's hand slipped from Quillen's shoulder as his eyes wandered back to the rolling expanse of the sea. 'My father told me she was spirited and brave. She loved to explore. She embraced her land-skin. Even though he found all he wanted in her, she...' His voice trailed off and he made no effort to capture it again.

He'd thought he had forgiven her. He'd thought the old grief, the loss and abandonment from those first seasons after his mother's disappearance, had been worn away, like stones smoothed by the tide. Instead, they'd simply sunk into the murky depths of his mind until time flung them up again on the shore. The old pain seared his chest, hot tears beading in his lashes.

'Fiadh is looking for answers too,' he continued. 'I can't say why, but I feel that if she finds hers, I'll find mine.'

Quillen raised his eyebrows. He rested back on his palms and tilted his head up to the sky.

'The pelt-stealer isn't your mother, Túathal.'

'I didn't say that.'

'What you *are* saying is just as nonsensical.'

Túathal sighed and bowed his head. 'Perhaps,' he murmured. 'But if there's a chance this is more than just a feeling… Quillen, do you believe the story of the moon and tide?'

'"The moon and tide dance with one another",' Quillen said, repeating a tale they'd both heard often as children, in song and in prose. 'I know the story, brother.'

'I feel like I'm the tide. Something moonlike is calling me to follow a dance I don't know the steps to, but as long as I follow her, no matter how many times I misstep or fall back, I will find what I need to find.'

'And the pelt-stealer is your moon, Túathal?'

Túathal made no answer and Quillen abruptly sat forward, jostling his friend by the shoulder. 'Do *you* know the story of the blinking star?'

Túathal snorted. 'That's a human warning—'

'Yes. Beware, you're in dangerous waters!'

'You think Fiadh is dangerous?'

'I think you're lost and confused, brother,' Quillen said with feeling, gripping Túathal's arm. 'Be wary.'

Standing, he pulled Túathal up with him. He moved towards the sea, but hesitated, looking over his shoulder into Túathal's hopeful face. He turned and embraced him.

'Be wary,' he repeated in Túathal's ear. 'But if you feel answers rest with this stranger… I truly hope you find them.'

11

BRENNA wasn't sure which struck first – the fever or the storm.

Once the Council had announced their decision, she'd felt weak. She'd assumed it was the effect of the long walk across Sjavaba on an injured leg, along with her carefully hidden anxiety about the Council's decision, abruptly released as their palms hit the high table. Without their protection, she'd dreaded to think what action the people might've taken against her.

But as she'd made her arduous way home, the weakness listed into aching, and the aching into shivers that chattered her teeth. She'd stumbled into her hovel and collapsed onto her nest before the dead fireplace. Despite the cold, she'd hauled off her coat and stripped to her underclothes, suddenly too hot.

The next thing she'd been aware of was the sound of heavy rain lashing the boarded windows, thumping in time with the pain in her head. Her neck and face had been hot to the touch, but at the same time she'd felt cold, her throat dry. Night had fallen and she could see nothing in the pitch blackness of her hovel.

Brenna knew she needed to light a fire, but her limbs were too heavy. She knew she needed water, food – she hadn't eaten for more than a day. But still, she couldn't rouse herself.

'I can't be ill,' she objected through stiff lips. 'I don't have time to be ill. They gave me a month, only a month…'

The fever dragged her through fitful, vivid dreams, flashing across her vision like the turns of the great lighthouse beacon before it'd been destroyed. Her father blazed against the darkness, tall and broad and gleaming with sweat. Alive. Then dead. Sjavaba's people jostled around her and she was small and they smiled and laughed, then leered, opening their mouths, and she was being devoured by wolves of every size and shape and colour, for Sjavaba's people were diverse in their heritage but not in their hatred. She wailed and stretched out her arms for her mother. And she was there. Lovely, doe-eyed.

'My baby,' she crooned in a tongue only they knew. 'Your skin is on fire. It's a terrible thing for your skin to burn.'

But before Brenna could prise her jaw open to speak, her mother was gone.

<h1 style="text-align:center">12</h1>

THE storm hadn't subsided even by the time Fiadh woke, though at first she barely heard it over her own ragged breaths. She found herself sprawled on the threshold. The door sagged even more on its hinges, the wolf's frustration gouged across its wood. Splinters pricked her fingertips.

She closed her eyes. The wolf exhausted her. Used her body, kept her mind awake and alert through the hours of the night, stretching it with richer, deeper senses. And when it withdrew at last, its strength sapped from her limbs, leaving her weak as a ragdoll.

The clamour of her breath quieted and she at last heard the rain. Then, of course, she had to get up. The lighthouse had no well that she'd found, so she ought to use the opportunity to collect rainwater.

Fiadh dragged herself off the floor and crossed to the scullery nook, staggering as though the slate floor were the deck of a storm-tossed ship. She lurched into the bench, jarring her ribs. Grasped a grungy pot and carried it with her outside. Crouched under the eaves to catch water running off the sloping roof. Scrubbed at the pot with her fingernails and set it in the open, the rain ringing metallically as it struck its bottom. Fiadh cupped her hands under the dripping stream and drank.

'Woman! What game do you think you're playing?'

The shout exploded behind Fiadh. She sprang to her feet so quickly she overbalanced, only just catching herself on the doorjamb. She stared behind her, into the lighthouse's dim interior. Her heart skidded in her chest, her fingers biting into the jamb. Was the lighthouse showing her another vision? Another glimpse into its memories, of a different woman who'd worn two skins?

Fiadh edged over the threshold. She saw no one, but as she trailed around the edge of the room, she heard another voice, coming from the narrow door between the bed and the scullery. The door Fiadh hadn't yet opened, but supposed must lead to the beacon tower.

'No games,' the second voice spat, husky and feminine. 'You would deny me even *rain*, after everything you've taken from me? My skin has been so dry.'

As Fiadh passed the fireplace, two shadowy forms blossomed in front of the narrow door. A small, plump figure with hair that spilled like water to the floor. And beside her, towering two feet over her, a man. Indistinct and blurred, as if the lighthouse wished to scrub him from its memories.

The blurred man snatched the woman by her wrists. Fiadh gasped and started forward, but the figures flickered, vanishing as abruptly as they'd appeared. The wind howled, rain battering the scullery windows, gusting down the chimney, stirring the ash in the hearth.

Nerves rattled, Fiadh moved to the narrow door and opened it. It was even colder and darker in the tight, circular room. A staircase curved away to the left, hugging the wall as it spiralled skyward.

As she paused in the doorway, a peal of thunder crackled outside, so loud the lighthouse groaned with the force of it.

She crossed her arms over her chest to stifle a shiver, the scrubbed-out image of the man embossed behind her eyelids. As she'd begun to realise when she'd swum with Dula and the rest, when she'd spoken with Túathal, the selkie woman from the visions hadn't freed herself from her second skin.

It had been stolen from her.

Stolen, like Fiadh's own wolf pelt.

'Are you really trying to help me?' she whispered dully. 'Or are you cursing me?'

⌘

Long, restless days followed.

The storm grew wilder, imprisoning her in the lighthouse. The lighthouse that breathed and dreamed old, old dreams.

She heard the wind sigh in its chimneys. Felt its timbers creak and settle, like the groaning of some great fretful creature. As the storm showered the lighthouse incessantly with sleet, buffeted it with wind and salt spray tossed high by the raging, riled sea, its memories echoed around Fiadh. Images and sounds and snatches of conversations from times lost to memory.

The selkie woman flitted across the room, appeared suddenly on the bed, moved in the scullery, lit the fireplace with uncertain fingers. Fiadh followed her, lost her, found her again. At times her eyes were fierce and she held herself as one ready to fight for her freedom. But more and more, as the days dragged on, her spirit withered and her eyes grew dull and sad.

Sometimes, she sang. Soft and low. Breathy, with a sob in her voice. Never as happily, as freely, as she had in the arms of her lover on the glitter-sand beach. She disappeared once up the beacon-tower stairs, setting her feet on steps that had long since rotted through and collapsed. Fiadh hadn't found the courage to follow her up to the tower, not while the storm howled around her. The lighthouse rarely conjured the man, but whenever Fiadh caught his towering shadow, the smudged edges of his hostile frame, she recoiled, condemnation piercing her heart.

With the barrage of visions and the wolf's desperate attempts to escape the prison of the lighthouse, Fiadh barely slept. When she did, her dreams were of a stocky girl with a mass of fiery hair, bite marks cruelly rent on her arms and legs and belly. Of a wiry man whose gentle hands held a knife that dripped blood onto a snow-white pelt. Of seals playing in peaceful, tumbling water, until the tide turned to smash them against tusk-like rocks.

On the sixth day, the storm swelled until Fiadh almost believed it would rip the lighthouse apart, stone by stone. She lay curled on the bed, arms flung over her head as if to hold it together while the splitting thunder cracked above. The wailing of the wind through the lantern room, its shrieking down the hollow beacon tower, sounded to her like the cries of the dead. The fire in the hearth cast pitching shadows over the walls. And in the sounds of this last surge, she heard the echoes of men blindly fighting the sea.

Then, all of a sudden, the storm died. The lighthouse stilled as if with a great sigh. Pale, washed-out light glowed against the scullery windows and lit faint diamonds across the slate.

Fiadh sobbed with relief. But it wasn't a relief, any more than waking with blood staining her teeth.

13

BRENNA woke abruptly and noticed the change at once. She knew by the heavy silence that the sleet and rain had stopped.

The change was in herself as well. Her fever had broken.

Flailing free from her blankets, she reached for the bucket of water she'd managed to fill on the second day of her fever. She plunged her hands into the bucket and splashed her face, cupped water in her palms and drank. Awkwardly, she rose and limped to her boarded window. A soft wind whistled through the gaps and she felt it brisk on her cheek, refreshingly cool. The world outside was painted in the cool tones of early morning, swathed in mist.

Brenna leaned against the table and carefully peeled her sweat-damp nightshirt from her injured arm. She grimaced at the inflamed skin and bruising mottled around her stitches.

'Great,' she muttered. 'Almost a whole week wasted and I need to see Yuel *again*. That stupid wolf could be anywhere by now.'

She hurried into her clothes and threw on her coat. Unhooking her lantern from its nail by the fireplace, she set it on the table, took the matches from the mantelshelf and bent to check its oil before lighting the cloth wick. She flicked the spent match into the fireplace and replaced the glass globe over the yellow tongue of flame.

Brenna unbolted the door with her elbow, one hand occupied with the lantern and her crutch hitched under the other. She wrestled the door open and stepped out into the rain-slicked street. Her feet sank into the shallow mud, unhelpful for her stiff legs, as she navigated

71

her way through the blue-grey gloom up a network of backstreets. The Council's official protection couldn't shield her from unwelcome eyes.

By the time she reached the apothecary's medicine house, the sun's light was brushing Sjavaba's tallest roofs and the sky had paled to peach. She snuffed her lantern, paused to hang it from her belt, climbed the steps and let herself in, cautiously poking her head around the door. Gloom shrouded the medicine house, but for the sparse flickering glow of candlelight. A match flared to life, drawing her eyes to the tall, narrow shadow to the left of the house. Dull light caressed Bo's sharp features and lit a spark in his eyes as he tended to the candles.

Brenna clacked her crutch sharply on the polished floorboards. Bo started and fumbled the match with a curse. Wincing, he turned to see who had disturbed him. His expression faltered for just a second, before his lips twitched to sour distaste and he looked down his nose at Brenna.

'What was that in aid of, please?'

'Was it you who loosed the Council on me?' Brenna snapped, lurching over the threshold.

Bo pressed his hands to his chest in an attitude of incredulity. 'Me? Why would I do that?'

'To see my end, I expect.'

He snorted. 'You're making that seem a favourable alternative at present, Brenna. But no, you can't credit me a part in spreading word to the Council. Though if I knew the pretty mess you'd make of it—'

'Pretty mess?' Brenna exploded. 'What do you know of it, then, turncoat?'

'Excuse *you* – oh wait, they didn't. Because you just had to make it all *worse* for yourself!'

Brenna gritted her teeth. 'I defended myself! I did what I had to—'

'No, all you *had* to do was keep your head low, stroke their vanity, plead for your life and let it all blow over. I can't believe you were stupid enough to challenge the Council!'

'Well, maybe if someone had my back, I wouldn't have to be so reckless!'

Bo drew up short, opening his mouth as if to protest. She knew as well as he did that he had no words to counter that strike. No argument that could absolve him in her eyes.

He pressed his lips into a hard line.

'Is someone there, Bo?' the apothecary's thin voice called, muffled. The door tucked behind the service counter opened and Yuel peered in. 'Ah. It's you. What is it this time?'

'I've had a fever, *apótekari*.' Brenna brushed past Bo as the old man shuffled out from behind the counter. 'I'm better now, but I'm concerned about my stitches...'

Nodding, Yuel took her by the arm and led her to the partitions. Brenna glanced back at Bo as she was ushered behind the screen. He wouldn't meet her eyes as he snatched up the box of matches and stalked out of sight.

Yuel led her to a cot. He nudged her shoulder and she sat down heavily.

'Let's have a look at those stitches,' he murmured, more to himself than her, Brenna thought. She began taking off her coat as the apothecary pottered around, collecting bandages, ointment, and a tiny pair of scissors.

After pouring a bowl of water from a pitcher on the bedside cabinet, Yuel drew up a stool beside her. He peered at her through the corner of his eyes. 'We get such terrible storms nowadays.'

Brenna paused in the middle of unbuttoning her sleeve. 'We've always had harsh winters, haven't we?' she replied, a wary edge to her voice.

'Yes,' he said. 'But they never used to flood Sjavaba. I heard the tide came quite far into the southern district this week.'

'Well, it didn't touch my house.'

'Interesting.'

Brenna stared at the old man. '*Apótekari*. Do you… do you believe I bear a curse in my blood? Like everyone else?'

He didn't answer, busying himself with arranging his tools on the bedside cabinet.

'You know me. You've known me since I was a baby!'

'Yes.' The old man lifted his eyes and looked straight into hers. He was so close she could see the russet colour of his irises. 'I delivered you, Brenna. I know better than most what sort of man your father was, what sort of… woman your mother was. So I know,' he continued, tapping the side of his narrow nose, 'just what sort of forces your father was playing with. I wouldn't be surprised if you were another facet of his curse.'

Brenna fumbled with the last few buttons of her shirtsleeve, slipping her injured arm free so he could see the discoloured wound.

'I hate my father, Yuel.'

'So does the sea, it would seem,' he said, a tiny pair of scissors in hand. 'And whatever war you wage against him takes Sjavaba down with it.'

Brenna gripped his wrist. 'I don't wage anything against my father. He's dead. He's paid the price for what he did, and I don't want revenge for that either, Yuel. I just want to leave this place. Why is that so hard for everyone to believe?'

The apothecary pulled his arm gently from her grasp and leaned closer to her stitches. The black threads showed starkly against her bare bruised skin. Brenna braced her shoulders and set her jaw, preparing for the discomfort ahead.

'The thing is, Brenna,' Yuel said, without taking his eyes from his work, 'you were never the sort of person to back down and flee. You got that stubbornness from your father, I'd wager.' He tugged a thread loose and Brenna winced.

'Well,' she muttered through stiff lips. 'Perhaps it's time I take after my mother. She knew when to get out.'

'You think she got out?' He said it musingly, in a tone that chilled her to the bone. She thrust her chin up and glared at him.

'Of course she did!'

Yuel snipped another thread and drew it free. Brenna caught her breath with a gasp, as he turned to dispose of the stained suture.

'And that,' he said in his dry, languid voice, 'sounds just like your father.'

14

The wolf still clung to life when the hunter started skinning it, though he did not realise this. He sliced his wicked þlade down the centre line of the wolf's belly, from its jaw to its haunches, the cuts not much deeper than its skin. Had he not been poaching on a noble's estate, perhaps he would have seen that his spear had not immediately killed his quarry. Perhaps he would have used the knife quickly against the animal's soft throat to save it from more pain.

But the hunter was in too much haste to notice.

By the time he stripped the hefty white pelt from the carcass, the wolf had died, its amber eyes staring glassily into oblivion. He bundled the rich fur into a rucksack, glancing nervously over his shoulder, tossed it onto his back and ran.

He didn't see what became of the carcass. How it melted, shifted, changed, like clay remodelled in a sculptor's hands.

Long after the gently falling snow of late winter had blurred the hunter's footprints, the groundskeeper found a woman's bloodied body, crusted with snow crystals. Feathery snowflakes clung to the lashes of her staring amber eyes.

She was a feywalker, though the hunter had not taken the time to recognise it. Nor did he learn for years yet that the curse of her unrighteous death clung to the pelt he had sliced from her still-warm body.

But when the time came and he draped the weighty pelt around

his young daughter's shoulders, he knew some of its power.
Enough to value it, but not to fear it.

15

FIADH moved with a silence cultivated by her cursed pelt. She felt every texture and contour of the frosted ground against the pads of her paws. Each scent wove together, rich and earthy, tangy and flat, into an intricate tapestry. She knew she could pull on any thread in that tapestry and trace it through the wood to its source.

I had to turn this time, she reasoned. *I haven't eaten in almost a week. I haven't the means or the time to set traps and this is the fastest way to root out any hare or fowl that might be around.*

She had given into the temptation quickly, briskly, determined not to see it as temptation at all. It was a necessity. The last thing she wanted, but the only way forward. And with her nose overfull with the perfume of the snow-flecked plain and every kind of tree in the nearing woods, with faraway shufflings and scratchings and whinings humming in her ears, she had little room to worry about the selkies.

If the storm had tested her sanity within the suffocating mystery of the lighthouse walls, how bad had it been for Túathal and his people? She'd heard the waves crashing and thundering. And when finally she'd been able to burst out of her prison and run down to the beach, the quarter moon faint in the pale morning sky, she'd seen the tide mark stained high up the basalt cliff.

Had monstrous waves crushed those ethereal creatures? Or had they left long before, taking with them any possibility of unravelling the answers she so desperately wanted?

The beach had been deserted. Though Fiadh had waited for

hours, pacing the black sands and twisting her fingers in taut fear, she'd seen no sign of the selkies. The water brides and grooms were nowhere on that beach, nowhere in the lacy foam. The ocean had purred demurely, as if it hadn't thrashed and wailed for days, hadn't beaten itself again and again on the basalt cliffs, frothing and white. Pounding as if to break them. As if to flood the land and swallow it up.

⌘

Fiadh tracked the hare in a winding trail through the tall grass and into the woods. The wolf's sharp teeth made short work of it and soon she melted into her more fragile frame, wiping her mouth with a scraggly tuft of the hare's fur. Her heart beat a little faster than normal, but with the fresh meat in her belly, she was revived. Almost sharp. She breathed in deeply, oriented herself, and started back the way she'd come.

Stretching out her hand, she let her fingertips brush the soggy wood of the black-barked trees. For a moment, under the skeletal boughs, winter stripped of their leafy dress, she could imagine she was back home. What she thought of as home, anyway.

Home had never been a place for her. It had always been a person.

Home was her father.

Sion had taught her woodcraft from a young age. They'd spent so much time in the wilderness of the land that she felt she could sense him among the trees. Could smell his stained hands in the scent of dripping sap. See his footprints alongside animal tracks. Hear his whistle in the wind and the rustle of bird wings. Feel his embrace, ever-present, in the heavy folds of the pelt against her skin.

He had always been a slight man. Shorter than most, with a wiry and nimble build. He was soft-spoken and gentle with her, though she knew him to be a skilled hunter.

Most clearly, she pictured his hands. Rough-skinned, bony, and scarred. Fingernails crusted with dirt and grime. Working deftly as he mended clothes or sharpened his hunting knives. Hovering over her own soft hands as he taught her how to tie a knot, how to wield a knife. How to skin an animal.

Fiadh stopped short, suddenly alert. She sank into a wary crouch, head tilted up. Just on the fringe of her senses, she heard movement in the undergrowth. Not the light skip of a rabbit or the rustling of birds. Heavier. She breathed in, running her senses over that rich tapestry, a little fainter in her human skin but still within reach, to find the one significant thread. A hint of oil. The lingering taint of smoke. A sharp counterpoint of blood—

She knew that scent. Knew that blood.

Fiadh froze. Stupidly. Like prey. She felt she should run, like she had the first time she'd stumbled upon her victim. Get away, lest the other girl's blood rouse the wolf slumbering within.

But the sun shone pale through the latticework of branches. Fiadh had ownership of her mind. And curiosity stirred in her. What was this girl doing out in the woods, so far from the town? Was she foraging? Hunting? Why so soon after receiving her injuries?

Fiadh ducked into the undergrowth and held herself still, waiting and watching. As the sounds of movement grew louder, she noticed that the girl moved with a limping gait. She bit her lip, shifting carefully around until she caught sight of the other girl, her mane of hair loose down her back. As she moved, the girl stopped abruptly and turned on her heel.

Their eyes met. Violet and honey-brown.

They stared at one another for a long moment. Fiadh realised she was holding her breath and let it out in a soft sigh. The other girl blinked. Rubbed her eyes. Glanced around, then back down at Fiadh.

'What are you doing here?' she asked.

Fiadh emerged slowly from the underbrush, dusting her shoulders and hair free of twigs and stray dirt, never taking her eyes from the red-haired girl.

'Walking.'

'Walking,' the other girl repeated. She frowned, before her eyes widened in recognition. 'You're the girl from the *apótekari's* shop. Why did you run out? Wait, have—' She stepped forward, glancing around them. 'Have you been out here all this time?'

Fiadh took a step back, eyes wide and wary.

The red-haired girl stopped her advance and drew back a little. 'Sorry,' she said stiffly. 'You've heard what they're saying about me then. It's utter tripe, but I won't convince you otherwise.'

Fiadh blinked. She shook her head. 'No…'

'No?' The disbelief was sharp in the girl's voice. She eyed Fiadh curiously. 'I'm Brenna,' she said at last, as if that would clarify her previous statement.

'Fiadh.'

'No, Brenna—'

'No. *My* name is Fiadh.'

'Oh.' A smile sprung across Brenna's face. Her hand flew to her mouth, as if the smile had exposed her in some way.

'What are *you* doing out here?' Fiadh ventured, emboldened by this flicker of humour.

Brenna's hand fell automatically to her right shoulder. 'Have you seen a white wolf?'

Fiadh flinched. 'A what?' she rasped, her chest suddenly tight.

'You didn't see it when you ran out of the *apótekari's* shop?' Brenna pressed. 'About a week ago, there was a wolf roaming the streets. I… have an arrangement with the Council. I need to find it.'

'You're hunting it,' Fiadh breathed.

Brenna eyed her closely. 'Um, Fiadh?' she said in a marginally gentler tone. 'Do you have somewhere to stay? You've not been out in the woods this whole time, have you? It's not safe.'

'No, no. I've… got somewhere to stay.'

Brenna nodded. 'Good. It'd be bad if the wolf attacked you. Or if you'd been caught in that storm—'

'Are you all right?' Fiadh interrupted, wringing her hands. 'You were attacked by the wolf you're looking for, right?' She bent her head, afraid to meet Brenna's eyes. 'Last time I saw you...'

Silence met her fumbling question. Biting her tongue, she glanced up. Brenna was staring at her, eyebrows knit together. 'I'm as well as can be expected,' she said slowly. 'Thanks. For caring.'

Fiadh untwisted her fingers and stared at the sickles of grime crusted underneath her nails. 'I'm so sorry. For what happened to you.'

'There's no point apologising for it!' Brenna burst out, so suddenly that Fiadh jumped. 'It's no one's *fault*. A wolf got into the town. It happens. The wolf attacked someone. It happens! No need to blame anyone for it. It was just a crazed wild animal and I was in the wrong place at the wrong time.' Frustrated tears sprang into her eyes. 'But no! That's not good enough for those people.' She began pacing agitatedly. 'It's all an omen. A *reckoning*. And of course, who else would be at the centre of it than—' Grunting, she kicked out at a tree. Its branches shivered and a shower of water fell on her.

Fiadh caught her by the arm before she overbalanced on the slick earth. Her smoky scent overwhelmed Fiadh's nostrils.

'I don't understand you,' Fiadh said. 'Who are they blaming for the wolf?'

Brenna tossed her damp hair. She met Fiadh's eyes, her own aglow with a low-burning fire. 'Me.'

'How could you have anything to do with it?'

Brenna flung up her arms. 'Everything's my fault! Or, everything was my father's fault. So, since he's dead, who else can they blame but me?'

'What did your father do?' Fiadh asked, voicing the question without even hesitating to think it tactless.

Brenna stepped back and rubbed her mouth, looking away. Fiadh sensed the other girl had opened up more than she'd meant to. Perhaps more than she had in a long time. But after only a brief pause, Brenna shrugged and moved closer, the fire sparking in her irises. She placed her hands on Fiadh's narrow shoulders and leaned invasively close.

'He angered the tide and incited a curse as deep as the ocean itself.' Her conspiratorial whisper resonated in the cold, still air. She scoffed. 'That's what they say.'

Fiadh swallowed, eyes wide.

'Yes,' Brenna breathed. She seemed to revel in the retelling, as if the story had burned, low but relentless, within her for too long. 'Oh, he was a good man once, they say. Always friendly, always grinning. Charming in his youth. But he harboured a dangerous fascination with the deep and it corrupted him.' She laughed, an angry, bitter sound. '*That* corrupted *him*. If anything, *he* corrupted *it*. But then, they never cared what he did in the isolation of the lighthouse, did they? Yes!' she exclaimed, misunderstanding Fiadh's alarm. 'No one expected the man who kept the beacon lit and warned sailors of danger would do what he did.' She dug her fingers into Fiadh's flesh. Leaned even closer to whisper in Fiadh's ear. 'He invoked the wrath of the tide, so it broke its borders and ravaged our port, the whole southern half of Sjavaba. He incited a curse as deep as the ocean itself, and even after his death, no ship can come or leave without being swallowed up. The tide is still angry.'

Brenna let go of Fiadh's shoulders and took a step back. Fiadh gasped, released.

'That's what they say,' Brenna repeated, her fire dampened.

Fiadh stared at her wordlessly. Turned her head to look towards the coast, where she knew the lighthouse rested, though of course they were too far away to see it. Shook her head slightly.

'What did they do?'

She didn't want to know. Didn't want to know why she'd found the lighthouse abandoned, its floor covered in soot, its rafters blackened by a fire that had once blazed in its belly.

Brenna turned her back on Fiadh. 'They ransacked the lighthouse,' she replied dully. 'They broke the beacon mechanism, smashed the tower windows. And…' Fiadh saw her hands ball into fists. 'They threw my father from the top into the cursed tide.'

Fiadh covered her mouth. Her own father's face flitted unbidden through her mind. She screwed her eyes shut, but still she saw Sion falling, until she lost sight of him in the crash of frothy white waves.

'Hey, are you all right?' Brenna's alarmed voice sounded far away, muffled by the horror Fiadh's imagination had conjured. She felt something brush her shoulder and shuddered away, eyes flying open.

The woman from the lighthouse stared back at her, a twist to her melancholy mouth.

Blinking, Fiadh shook her head, shivering uncontrollably. Brenna caught her arms and tried to hold her still.

'What's the matter with you?' she demanded.

Fiadh scrabbled at the other girl's arms, chest pounding. She cast wildly about, but the vision had vanished.

'Hey, hey!' Brenna cupped Fiadh's face in her hands. 'It happened a long time ago. Don't—'

'What does it mean?' Fiadh hissed feverishly. 'It has to *mean* something!'

Brenna snorted. 'People are vile. Wicked. That's all it means.'

'No!' Fiadh shook her head, tearing free from Brenna's grasp. Barely knowing what she wanted to hear. Of course she knew the wickedness of people. But the hands that'd torn skin from flesh had also held her safe and warm. There had to be more to the lighthouse's story. If not, how would she free herself from the wolf? She would choose human wickedness over the mindless savagery of her pelt—

Would you?

'Fiadh, you're unwell,' Brenna said firmly. She looked up at the sky and clicked her tongue. 'We should get you somewhere warm and dry, all right?'

Back to the town, packed wall to wall with people?

Fiadh shuddered. If she were dragged in, she wouldn't be let out again. Night would come, and with it the wolf. Brenna would see the curse of her pelt. And the wolf would again fall to a hunter's blade.

Fiadh clutched Brenna's hands and squeezed them in hers, noting their work-worn texture.

'I'm sorry, Brenna,' she whispered. It was all she could say.

She turned on her heel and fled.

16

'YOU'RE back!' Dula squealed, almost knocking Fiadh over with the force of her embrace. She clasped Fiadh's hands and skipped her in a playful circle. 'Did you come to swim with us again?'

'Dula!' Fiadh gasped, already breathless from her climb, now reeling in the grip of the selkie woman's overwhelming energy. 'You're safe!'

'Why wouldn't I be, dear?'

'The storm.' Fiadh gestured to the basalt cliff. 'The tide mark is most of the way up the cliff – this beach must've been completely flooded! Where did you go?'

Dula smiled. 'There are always nooks and coves we can shelter in,' she replied carelessly, as if fears for her safety shouldn't have plagued Fiadh for the better part of a week, nearly twisting her nerves to break.

Fiadh nodded slowly, soaking it in. They were alive. They were all right.

Craning to look over Dula's head, she searched the cluster of selkies milling on the shore. Their speckled, striped, patchy forms mingled in the foam, playing tricks on her eyes. She caught a glimpse of silver and let go of Dula's hands. As she started falteringly across the sand, Túathal's silver head turned. His face lit up. She wet her lips to call out to him.

'Túathal—'

He sprang up the sands and flung his arms around her, lifting her off her feet. Her toes brushed the sand and she tripped backwards a step.

'Fiadh!' he exclaimed, grinning broadly. 'You came back!'

'I had to,' she croaked, swallowing against the stinging sensation at the back of her throat. 'When the storm ended, I couldn't find you. I thought the storm must have… or that you'd left, or…' She pressed a palm to his chest and gently pushed him away, swiping at her eyes with the heel of her other hand. 'But you're all right. I needn't have feared for you at all.'

Túathal bent his head to peer at her. 'You were afraid?'

Fiadh lifted her face to his, to those liquid eyes, penetrating in their innocent concern. As clueless as Dula, as perhaps his whole clan, to the fear that seethed in her chest and constricted her lungs. Constant. Oppressive.

She clasped her hands to still their shaking. The gathering of selkies churned all around her, like calm waters lapping about her petrified form.

She should've expected it, she realised, as she watched them play and dance, shifting forms to frolic in the waves. She should've known they couldn't understand her fear. Her lips trembled. 'Oh, yes, Túathal. So very afraid.'

'The pelt-stealer.'

Fiadh jumped. A black-brown water groom, a head taller than the rest, was approaching them. There was something hard about his face that she hadn't observed in the others. A stern look in his eyes. A firm set to his mouth.

Fiadh shrank behind Túathal, half-dropping to a wary crouch. The stranger fixed her with a dark look, before raising his eyebrows at Túathal.

'So she did come back.'

Fiadh's chest resonated with the depths of his voice. 'I'm sorry?' she faltered. She glanced at Túathal, unsure what she should say, what she'd done… 'Wait, *pelt-stealer?*'

'Quillen!'

Dula hopped up beside her groom and butted her head affectionately against his arm. Quillen blinked and looked down at her, his face softening. She wrapped her arms around his middle and rested her chin on his shoulder, smiling up at him. 'You've met the other sort of skin-changer.'

'Yes,' he agreed warmly. He swept her long hair back from her face and bent to kiss her forehead. She giggled.

Hesitating, Quillen looked back at Túathal. Fiadh watched them curiously, biting her lip. But at last, Quillen sighed and took Dula's hand.

'Swim with me?'

Dula laughed, spinnning around and reaching for Fiadh. 'Join us!'

Fiadh gave a startled shake of her head.

'Come, Dula,' Quillen urged. 'Let us leave… the *other* sort of skin-changer alone.'

Dula pouted but followed her groom into the surf. The couple drew their hoods over their heads and vanished beneath the waves.

Fiadh watched them until they were out of sight, before turning to Túathal. 'You told him about my pelt,' she said, a sour taste in her mouth.

'Yes. I talked to him after we spoke.'

'He doesn't like me.'

'He doesn't *trust* you,' Túathal corrected. A little too brightly, Fiadh thought.

'Why?'

Túathal opened his mouth, but then closed it again, glancing around at his clan. He touched Fiadh's elbow and drew her away, down to the western edge of the crescent beach. Fiadh noticed the narrow crevice half-submerged by the tide. The sea cave would be flooded.

'Pelt-stealers aren't unheard of,' Túathal said in a conspiratorial whisper. 'Some of our older clanmates tell stories about them. They want us to be wary.'

'You don't seem very good at that.'

Túathal laughed. 'No. Especially not at this season. Everyone's too excited for worries like that.'

'This season?'

Túathal gestured to his people. 'We're here for the bridal season. You see? No elders or children. We left them at our islands in the moonset oceans. For hundreds of generations, we've come to this shore for the bridal season. It's a sacred place.'

Fiadh looked again over the neat crescent of the beach and tilted her head, seeing it with fresh eyes. 'It looks like a young moon,' she murmured.

'Yes,' Túathal grinned. 'It represents the phase of life we're living. Still young, but waxing bigger and bigger. And it's a cycle. Like the moon, our generations wax and wane. There will always be new grooms and brides to join the dance.'

Fiadh smiled. 'I see.'

'Fiadh,' Túathal said, dragging her attention away from his people. 'Do you... know of any other selkies? Anyone who might look like one of us' – he gestured to his people, to himself – 'who lives on the land?'

'You're the first selkies I've met,' Fiadh began automatically. She blinked. 'Except...'

Túathal leaned closer. 'Except?' he prompted, eyes wide and eager.

Fiadh nibbled her lip, unsure of what to say. 'I've seen... visions.' He stared at her blankly. 'When the wolf brought me here, I found shelter in the old lighthouse.' She pointed upwards. 'You can almost see it from here. It's on this cliff. The lighthouse has been... I know it sounds strange. But the lighthouse has been showing me a woman. Visions of a selkie woman. And sometimes I can hear her sing and she sings like you.'

Túathal grabbed her shoulders. Fiadh started, alarmed by the intensity of his expression.

'A woman?' he repeated. 'What does she look like?'

Fiadh didn't need to pause to think about it. She'd seen the woman so many times in the past week that she could recall almost every aspect of her, from her long-lashed black eyes and floor-length hair to her dappled skin and soft figure.

But she did pause. Her eyes widened and she stared Túathal over. The silver of his skin and hair, the fawn patches on his arms and jaw. It was like seeing him for the first time.

'She looks like you,' she breathed. 'Túathal, who… who is she?'

Túathal tore away from her. 'Show me!' he shouted. He set his hands on a ledge above his head and tried to clamber up the cliff.

'She's a vision,' Fiadh said, running to join him. He lost his footing and skidded back down. 'She's not really there!'

'Then maybe I can see her too!' Túathal again tried to haul himself up the cliff, only to drop down.

'Stop it! You'll hurt yourself.'

'Fiadh, I need to see her.' He spun around and grasped her arm. 'Last time we spoke, I realised I didn't just come here for the bridal season. I did, but more than that, I need to know what became of my mother. And I knew – I just *knew* it! Knew that the answers were with you!'

'With me? Your… Túathal, you think that woman is your mother?'

'Yes! I mean, I can't be sure unless I see her.'

'What happened to her?'

'She disappeared when I was just a pup. My father could only guess she'd been killed, maybe by fishermen, or sharks. It happens. But I started to question that. My father, he said she was adventurous, spirited. Maybe, I thought, maybe she wanted to explore the land and try living among people. But maybe she got lost and couldn't come back to us. That was all just hope, a small boy's dream, though…' He trailed off. Raised his hand, as if to brush her face. Stopped and let it fall. 'You may have seen her.'

Fiadh searched his eyes, then looked over her shoulder, up to where she knew the lighthouse stood. 'So, the lighthouse isn't answering me?' she asked, unable to hide her disappointment. 'It's trying to answer you?'

Túathal ran a hand through his damp hair. 'I didn't mean… well. How could visions of my mother answer your questions?'

'She wasn't wearing her pelt,' Fiadh said. 'I thought maybe she'd…'

Túathal frowned, the expression ill-suited to his face. Fiadh sucked her lips and dropped her eyes.

'What?' he pressed. 'You thought she'd what?'

Fiadh ducked her head, hiding behind her waxen hair. 'Cast aside her pelt? Only at first.' Shaking herself, she set her chin and looked back into his face. 'No. Not after we last talked. Your life isn't like mine. You're born to both bodies, so why would she cast one away? When I saw her on the beach—'

'What?' Túathal's eyes bulged. 'You saw her? *Here?*'

'Yes.' Fiadh spoke low, looking beyond him to the brides and grooms. Many had again settled to rest on the higher sands. She could see a few seal heads skimming in the shallows, a few others playing and laughing. 'I saw her here the night you all arrived. She was dancing.' Her chest ached. She wished she could finish the story there and leave out the rest, for his sake. For her own. 'I thought maybe she'd given up her life as a selkie. I wanted to know how and whether that could help me. But she was smiling and laughing and clearly joyful among your people. In the lighthouse, she is always sad.'

Túathal's face fell. 'Sad?'

Fiadh wrung her hands. She didn't want to upset him, but if the silver-and-fawn woman was Túathal's mother, he had a right to know. 'Sad and angry, or scared.'

'That doesn't sound like her.'

Fiadh's fingers twitched to touch his hand. To give him some small comfort, after the dreadful wound she'd inflicted. 'All right,' she said instead, averting her eyes. 'I'll take you to the lighthouse. Listen,' she pressed, interrupting his exclamation of thanks. 'I can't promise you'll see anything. But yes, I'll take you.'

Túathal grinned. 'You're heaven-sent, Fiadh!' He caught her hands in his and kissed her knuckles. 'Thank you!'

17

TÚATHAL looked up from inspecting his grazed hands to see that Fiadh was leading him towards a tapering, battered structure. Rough-hewn stonework made up its walls. The top flashed dazzlingly, reflecting the light of the sun.

Blinking, he almost bumped into Fiadh. She'd stopped quite suddenly a few metres from the weathered door.

'Are you ready?' she asked. When she turned to look up at him, the peculiarity of her features struck him anew, as it had when he'd first found her in his arms. Her eyes, in particular – so narrow, compared to those he was used to seeing among his clan, and so delicately coloured. She stood before the door like an otherworldly spirit waiting to whisk him into another realm and reveal the mysteries of the ages.

Túathal tried to smile. Usually it was so easy, but his lips felt stiff with sudden unease. He nodded instead.

Fiadh smiled encouragingly and crossed the remaining distance to the door. Twisting the handle, she shoved the door inwards. It squealed harshly across the slate. Túathal clapped his hands to his ears and gritted his teeth, before leaning forward. The inside was dim as a cave.

'I'm sorry.' Fiadh stepped cautiously over the threshold. 'I don't have anything to light and haven't collected firewood…'

'Firewood?' Túathal repeated blankly. He followed her inside and allowed his gaze to wander around the interior of the building. The

93

structure and items within were strange and he couldn't guess their purpose.

'Oh, right. It's just wood that you collect to burn. Um, if you know what burning is?' Túathal flashed her an apologetic smile. 'Doesn't matter then. It's just that it's almost too dark to see in here.'

'No, it's not.'

'Really?' He felt Fiadh move close and looked down. A wondering smile played across her mouth. 'You must have very good eyes. But that makes sense, I suppose.'

'It…' For some reason, it was hard to speak. Wetting his lips, Túathal forced his eyes back to roaming the strange place. 'It gets darker than this in the sea.'

Fiadh touched his arm and pointed to a low, rectangular object made out of wood. 'I first saw her there,' she said. 'Sitting on the bed.'

Heart quickening with something akin to excitement, but more closely related to apprehension, Túathal took a tentative step towards the bed. They waited for a time, holding themselves stiffly, glancing around at intervals. The room remained distinctly absent of phantom mothers.

Fiadh's fidgeting fingers caught his eye. He reached out and took her hand. Though she flinched at his touch, she didn't pull away. Just looked up at him again and smiled sadly.

'I'm sorry. I don't know if she'll appear again. I shouldn't have raised your hopes.'

'It hasn't been too long,' he said. 'And perhaps she wasn't… I mean, we don't know…'

'No.'

'This place is strange.'

'Yes, you could say that. I haven't been in many buildings since I was given this pelt, but it's the strangest I've known.'

'I've not been in buildings.'

Fiadh giggled. A sweet burbling sound.

Relaxing, Túathal let his curiosity overtake his disappointment for the time being. 'Show me!' he exclaimed. He bounded into the centre of the room, bouncing on the balls of his feet as he spun, arms outstretched, grinning. 'What *is* this place? What is it for? Humans make things for reasons, don't they? I believe I've been told that.'

Fiadh giggled again and circled around him. He twirled on the spot to keep her in view as she paced the circumference of the room. 'It's a lighthouse...'

'But I don't know what that *means*, Fiadh,' he chided playfully.

'I was about to explain,' she said with mock severity and he laughed. 'The light is at the top – or, it's supposed to be. I haven't gone up there yet, but I heard it's broken. When it works, though, it shines a really bright light that can be seen from far away, so sailors in the dark know how close they are to land.'

Túathal gave a bark of delighted laughter. 'The blinking star!' he cried. '"Beware, you are in dangerous waters." We've heard of this signal. So this is where the star comes from! But how?' Túathal demanded, still turning in place, eyes fixed on Fiadh as she stepped a ring around him. 'It's not made of light and there's no light in here. You made that clear when we came in.'

'I don't know how they keep it burning, but when it works, there's a fire at the top and a mechanism that spins it around so it flashes. Or blinks.' She winked.

'What do you mean by fire? What is it like?'

Fiadh slowed her steps and touched her chin. 'I can show you,' she said thoughtfully. 'I just need a bit of kindling.'

'Kindling? So many new words, Fiadh. Where shall we find it?'

'We don't need to look far. Grass can be kindling, or twigs from trees. Anything dry and brittle, almost.' Her face was alight.

'And I'm confused again. How does it become fire?'

'You'll just have to wait, Túathal. Wait and watch. Let me show you.' She brushed past him, bidding him follow with a flicker of her dusky eyes, so close he saw the faint light catch in her lashes. He shadowed her back over the threshold. She took barely three steps before bending in the long grass, tearing feathery bouquets of the stuff. Rainwater sprayed her feet and she said something about it being too wet.

Back inside, she tugged a thread loose from the ragged cloth scattered over the slate and tied her bundle of grass. She hung it from a shelf above a blackened alcove, the purpose of which Túathal couldn't discern. Though she told him he'd have to wait a while, he didn't mind it, for while they waited, she spoke with him again. And now he knew she wasn't going to slip away, leaving him with more questions than before.

He watched her move with a quiet, gentle grace. Noticed the weary shadows cupped beneath her eyes.

Slowly, hesitantly, she spoke of her family. Of a near-sighted mother, a woodman father. Of the childhood she'd known, her hands held in the rough warmth of theirs. Opening the pouch that dangled from a knotted cord about her neck, she drew out a twist of butter-yellow hair and kissed it. Then a fine, tarnished chain with mangled links and a tiny pendant. A tight-rolled scroll of faded paper, faded ribbon, faded words. Each a story she shared of two people she'd loved and lost, in different ways. He heard in her words a time before. A time when she'd been more human. Less like himself, yet more like him, too.

She let him hold the chain. It reminded him of ships he'd passed under with his clan, of the anchors cast down on great steel links. But this was fragile, already broken. Then the scroll's creamy paper rustled drily in his fingers. And he could understand neither, for they came from humans. And he saw that Fiadh was human. Her pelt truly stolen, truly foreign to her.

Fiadh put the treasures back in her pouch and took out two grey objects. Something sharp and flat, something round and rough. She took the dry grass from where it hung and they knelt together before the alcove. Tossing the bundle into it, she took the grey objects and struck them against each other.

Yellow stars scattered and jumped. A glint of yellow caught the kindling. Fiadh blew gently, coaxing the fire to life. Túathal gasped and leaned close. Its heat flushed over his arms, his cheeks. It flared brightly, licking up the twist of grass. And as quickly as it'd flared, it died in a bed of grey ash, leaving everything dimmer than before.

Túathal's chest ached.

'It's not working. The blinking star, the lighthouse. It's not working.'

'No. It was broken.'

'How do the humans on their vessels know the waters are dangerous?'

'I suppose they don't.'

'Why hasn't it been… fixed?'

Fiadh sighed and leaned against him. She tilted her head up at the sloping ceiling. 'People are wicked,' she murmured. 'Maybe that's all there is to it.'

Túathal waited but she didn't elaborate. 'I don't understand,' he admitted at last. She only shook her head, as if too weary to explain.

'Can we see it?' he asked. Fiadh rolled her head and frowned at him. 'The light at the top.'

'Yes.' Fiadh nodded to herself. 'I've been meaning to, but… yes. We should.'

She got up and Túathal rose with her, following her through a narrow door and into a smaller room with a spiralling staircase. It was even dimmer in the tower than the rest of the house. She stepped aside so Túathal, with his sharper eyes, could take the lead. As he stepped in front of her, he felt her fingers pinch the back of his garment.

He held the rail tightly. When he glanced down the flight, an unfamiliar tightness constricted his chest. If the narrow, creaking beams beneath his feet gave way, he'd plummet to the slate floor below. The thought of freefalling without the support of the tide made him uneasy, though he didn't know the damage a fall like that might do.

They reached the landing. Fiadh's panting breaths echoed in the dimness and Túathal realised he too was breathing heavily. Fiadh's eyes sought his in the dark, but he could tell she couldn't quite make him out. He guided her hand to the door and she wrested it open. Honey-coloured light pooled around them.

A small flight of steps led up from the doorway and onto a round platform. Túathal blinked and raised a hand to shield his eyes. Sunlight was scattered across the floor, blazing sharply. Crouching down, he stretched out to touch a gleaming shard. Fiadh tugged at his shoulder and shook her head.

'It's glass,' she warned him. 'Sharp. Watch where you step.'

In the middle of the platform, a rippled prism stood on a central dais. Túathal saw, squinting through the dazzle of shifting rainbows, that the tall globe-like thing had been smashed in several places.

The circular room had no walls. A lattice-like structure of posts and beams encircled the room, supporting the domed roof. Several clouded, chipped panes still held their place within the latticework, but most of the frames were empty. A blustering wind keened through the exposed room, ruffling Túathal's hair and the fur of his pelt.

Beyond the latticework, Túathal could see a balcony. He stepped cautiously towards it, ducking out through a hole. The western sky blazed amber with the setting sun, the clouds dyed gold by its retreating rays.

His heart throbbed. A grin burst across his face and he gave a whoop of laughter. Laughter at the warm, golden beauty of it all. Laughter at the wind that swept about him like the currents of his own tides. He felt light again – light of body, but also of spirit.

'Your vision,' he called back to Fiadh, without taking his eyes from the brilliance of the western horizon, 'can't have been of my mother. She could never be unhappy here!'

'Túathal...'

'I can see the tide! It's so far below us, and the foam is yellow from the sun...' He braced his hands on the rail and leaned boldly over it. The wrought metal balustrade dug into his belly. 'The sea, Fiadh! It stretches on and on until it touches the sky—'

'*Túathal!*' Her voice was a shriek.

Túathal whipped around. She'd followed him to the latticework but had stayed on the inside. She was shaking. Her hands gripped the jagged edges of the beams, so hard her knuckles shone bone-white. A thin stream of blood glided down the metal and pattered on the floor. Fiadh had cut the palm of her hand on the shattered glass still crusted on its frame.

'Fiadh!' Túathal reached for her through the lattice. 'What's wrong?'

'Wolf,' she rasped through trembling lips. 'The wolf.' Her eyes were wide and glassy. The dusky violet of her irises looked almost amber in the sunset. 'It's waking!'

Túathal swung himself back through the gap and put his arms around her. She was shivering so violently. But she shoved him away and shook her head.

'Does it hurt you?' Túathal tried to brush the hair out of her face. He gasped with alarm. Her milky cheek was bristling with fine hairs, the hair on her head growing, cascading in a ridge down her neck to meet the pelt on her back. 'Fiadh?'

'Get out of here!' Fiadh roared. She twisted her neck. 'It's not safe! *I'm* not safe!'

Túathal backed away from her. The light, which had shone blindingly all about them only moments before, dimmed quickly, the shards of sunlight paling. The heel of his foot jarred on the lantern prism's raised dais. Fiadh's melting, shifting form cut a dark silhouette against the burned orange and crimson of the sunset sky.

'Fiadh…'

She crumpled in on herself. Túathal gasped and started forward.

A low growl rumbled through the room. For a bewildered second, Túathal thought it was the distant purr of thunder.

The dark shape hunkered where Fiadh had stood. It rose steadily.

Túathal froze.

He'd known nothing of the shape Fiadh had worn on the beach. But he could recognise a predator when it stared him in the face. And he did recognise it – in the creature's glowing eyes, in the gleam of its bared moon-pearl teeth.

In the rigid tension of its body. Poised to strike.

18

BRENNA let her front door slam shut and slid the bolt home.

She crossed to her pantry, mostly stocked with clouded jars of pickled eggs or vegetables. Taking a waxed cloth bundle from a shelf, she unwrapped it, tearing at the hunk of bread with her teeth. It was tough to chew. Too stale. She tossed the hunk onto the table, crumbs scattering over its surface. Wrenched her coat off her and let it fall onto the floor. Lit a fire in the hearth and leaned against the end of the table.

The wolf had vanished. No one had seen it for a week. Any tracks it may have left must've been washed away in the storm.

Brenna drummed her palms on the table edge. She turned and picked up the hunk of bread again. Ripped a bit off with her fingers and popped it into her mouth.

Not only had the wolf eluded her, but the mysterious girl had also disappeared. Brenna tried not to dwell on that. What business was it of hers what some wild stranger did? What did it matter to her that the girl was clearly distressed? Unwell? Perhaps in danger?

She threw back her head and screwed her eyes shut. Of course it mattered. Even if nobody else in this forsaken town cared that a young girl with no family or friends was fending for herself in the wild, it *had* to matter to Brenna.

Touching her tender shoulder, she winced. Not at the pain of her injury, but at the memory of the onlookers who'd found her bleeding out in the streets and had raised neither hand nor voice to help her.

There was something else. Something about that wild girl – Fiadh, she'd said her name was. Perhaps it was her fragile-looking frame, unthreatening and vulnerable. Or perhaps it was the simple fact that she, unlike so many others, had listened to Brenna. Whatever it was, there was some connection between them.

Brenna groaned in frustration and threw the last of the too-tough crust into the hearth. No matter how she felt about Fiadh, she couldn't do anything about it. Not since she'd lost her in the woods.

She grimaced. She was good at losing things.

From too young an age, Brenna had known that her mother was a prisoner. The lighthouse keeper had often taken Brenna to Sjavaba when he'd bartered for goods from merchants he'd helped guide safely to port. She'd often followed him through the fringes of the forest to collect wood for fire and carving. Her mother had always remained behind, but not because she liked her home. Idunn had hated the lighthouse. She'd told Brenna so.

On nights when her father had been working up in the beacon tower, ensuring the light remained lit and the lantern kept turning, her mother had held her close in their shared bed and spoke of the sea, her voice deep and syrupy thick. Brenna had nestled against her mother's soft body and played with her long, silky hair. Idunn had told her stories and sung her songs about creatures that lived in the tide, of underwater worlds where a clan of selkies thrived. When she and Brenna were alone, she had spoken to her in a language Brenna hadn't heard among the townspeople or the foreigners at the docks. A language all their own, she'd thought.

The lighthouse keeper hadn't locked Idunn inside with latch or key, but she'd been a prisoner all the same. Something else bound her to stay. Not love of the keeper. Brenna had learned, too young to be burdened with the knowledge, that Idunn didn't love him.

She'd thought her mother stayed for her. For the songs they'd sung together in the gathering dusk, Idunn braiding her daughter's vibrant red curls. For the stories Brenna had babbled about Sjavaba and the comings and goings of merchants and sailors. For the simple love a mother has for her daughter.

Yet, clearly, that love had not been her bondage.

One morning when she was still a child, Brenna had woken in an empty bed. She still remembered how the morning sun had streamed through the scullery windows, casting diamonds of mote-specked light on the slate. Her father had stood in the centre of the room, dripping salty water on the threadbare carpet, his hands and arms streaked with oily ash.

When he'd looked at her, she'd known that her mother was gone. That she had vanished into her beloved sea.

And that had only been the beginning of what Brenna would lose.

19

TÚATHAL backed up onto the lantern's dais, never taking his eyes from the snarling wolf that stood in Fiadh's place. It followed him, shadowing his steps, growling low in its throat. The light was fading fast.

'Fiadh,' he breathed. He edged around the lantern's shattered globe, the wolf's eyes unwavering upon him. 'Fiadh, it's all right. It's…'

He faltered. There was no intelligence behind those eyes. When he swam with his siblings among regular seals, he could tell them apart easily. There was humour in the faces of his kin, their deeper knowledge evident in their eyes and movement. It set them apart from the beasts they swam alongside.

Even though the creature before him shared a body with her, it wasn't Fiadh. Whatever mind used to possess the pelt did so no longer.

Túathal stopped backing away. He cocked his head to one side, fascinated. It was just an animal, running on instinct alone.

The wolf paced back and forth at the foot of the dais, teeth bared. Despite this, Túathal felt strangely calm.

'You're just scared, aren't you?' he crooned. The wolf growled. Túathal edged forward, holding out his hand. 'Fiadh is scared too. But I'm not going to hurt you. You see? You're safe.'

The wolf circled to the other side of the dais, as Fiadh had playfully paced around him only a couple of hours ago. Túathal skirted around the lantern globe to keep it in sight, glancing quickly over his shoulder. The door to the staircase was behind him. If he timed it right, he could put the lantern between himself and the wolf and make a run for it.

'But I'm not going to do that,' he murmured. He crouched on the dais and smiled. The wolf checked its pacing and stopped, eyeing him warily. 'I'm not going to leave you alone like this, Fiadh.'

The wind changed direction. Túathal tilted his head. Ever so faintly, he heard voices. His clanmates on the shore had started singing their evening songs. The wolf's ears pricked and it closed its mouth.

Túathal licked his lips. Took a breath, unsure whether what he was about to do would work, and started to sing. Soft and husky. A song that ebbed and flowed with a steady, calming rhythm. The wolf raised its head, no longer poised in a half-crouch. It stepped closer. And, after Túathal had sung the song twice through, the wolf lowered itself onto its belly and rested its head on its paws.

Still singing, Túathal shuffled closer. He reached out a hand. The wolf bared its teeth. Túathal paused, lowered his lashes, and bowed his head.

The wolf relaxed. Túathal touched the long creamy fur on the top of its head, and when it didn't protest, ran his hand along its neck, losing his fingers in the rich coarse fur.

'That's it.' He stroked the thick white pelt. 'You're no monster. Just scared. Isn't that right?'

The wolf snuffed, closing its eyes. Túathal chuckled softly and started another song, a song from his childhood. A song that tasted of sea salt and long green grass. A song that resonated off grey rocks and hissed like foam on shale beaches. A song warm with the arms of a mother crossed tight around her young pup.

Another voice joined with his.

Túathal's hand stiffened in the wolf's fur. A shiver ran through him. The words of the song stuck to his suddenly dry tongue, but the other voice didn't falter.

He knew that voice.

Slowly, ever so slowly, so as not to break whatever spell this might be, he turned to look over his shoulder. Standing before the flight of stairs that led down to the tower door was a woman. A woman dappled fawn and silver, wearing a white shift that billowed gently around her ankles.

She didn't seem to notice Túathal and the wolf on the other side of the dais. As she moved across the circular room towards the latticework wall, Túathal opened his mouth to cry a warning. The glass – but it didn't seem to bother her. Her feet glided across the platform as if there were no glass at all. She moved through the latticework and stepped onto the balcony.

Túathal rose to follow her, carefully avoiding the glass. Breathed in shakily and slipped back through the gap to join her.

She was so much smaller than he remembered. Or rather, he was so much taller than when he'd last seen her.

He stared at her profile. Her black eyes were fixed on the horizon, her dappled cheeks wet, tiny droplets clinging to her long lashes. He covered his mouth as tears pricked in his own eyes.

She was singing for home. Singing for *him*.

'Mamma…' He moved to grasp her shoulder. 'Mamma, it's me. It's—'

Túathal's hand passed through empty air and jarred on the metal railing.

He stared at the space where the memory of his mother had stood. His ears strained for the echoes of her song, but the air was silent.

He crumpled to the floor and wept.

FIADH turned under the blanket. It was deliciously warm, if musty. Eyes closed, she breathed in deeply through her nose.

Fresh snow and old ash. The faraway traces of wood smoke. The deep salt scent of the ocean, roaring not far off. And, interlaced with the wolf's heady musk, the oceanic aroma she now knew belonged to the selkies.

'Túathal…'

She opened her eyes. Blinked. Pushed back the covers and sat up. She was lying in the lighthouse bed. From the angle of the light on the threadbare rug, she guessed it was long after sunrise. She hadn't slept so well for months. Gathering the blanket, she swathed herself with it and slid off the bed. The slate tiles were freezing under her feet.

'Túathal?' she called. The trailing blanket stirred ash and dust in her wake. She sneezed and looked around the dim, draughty room, but couldn't see her friend. She frowned. She could *smell* him, though. 'Túathal?'

How had she gotten into bed? She couldn't remember… no. Pursing her lips, she tried to mentally retrace her steps. She'd taken Túathal up to the lighthouse. They'd climbed the stairs and entered the lantern room, but she hadn't realised it was so close to evening. She'd assured herself there was still time. The sun hadn't set. She would be able to send Túathal away before the wolf woke…

Fiadh stopped in the middle of the rug.

But there hadn't been enough time. The familiar, dreaded

sensation of the wolf had risen within her, the pelt crawling over her skin, even as Túathal had lost himself in the brilliance of the sunset.

'Túathal!'

She ran her tongue over her teeth. Checked her hands. Looked down at the clean white of the wolf's pelt. But where was he?

'*Túathal!*'

'Fiadh?'

She spun around. Darted for the doorway to the stairs, thrust back her head so that she could see the landing. Heard a scuffle and slither above her. Then Túathal's head peered over the balustrade.

Letting out a bark of laughter, he disappeared. She heard his bare feet clatter down the flight of stairs, accompanied by the rustling hiss of his trailing garment. He swept down the final rung and caught her in a hug.

'You're awake!'

Fiadh opened her mouth to ask what'd happened after the wolf had awoken. Had it attacked him? Why hadn't he fled when she'd told him to? Why was he *still* here? But he'd already dashed away to the scullery.

Fiadh stumbled after him. Rattling the window latch, he pushed a panel open, a shower of snow slithering free. He shoved his head out and breathed in the white frosty air. She came up behind him.

'What… what happened last night?'

Túathal pulled back from the window. His fawn fingers fumbled with the latch, his shoulders hunched, until it finally rasped into place. Yet still he didn't face her.

'Why aren't you looking at me?' She could hear her voice rising despite herself. 'Did I hurt you? Oh Túathal, I—'

'No. No…'

She tried to circle around him to see his face. 'Then why…?' He twisted around, shielding himself with his hands. 'Túathal! Why won't you look at me?'

For a heart-stopping second, she saw Brenna, angry red bleeding through her clothes in the smoky gloom of the apothecary's shop.

She grabbed Túathal's wrists and pulled his hands away, her blanket slipping to the floor. His dark eyes were red-rimmed. Tears clung to his lashes and left glistening tracks down his blotchy cheeks. There was not a scratch on him.

'I saw her,' he rasped.

'Saw her? The woman?'

'Yes. My mother. She was crying.'

'Oh.' Fiadh bit her lip. She wanted to press him for answers about the wolf, but he was clearly in distress. Swallowing her questions, she bent to pick up the blanket, before taking his hand and drawing him over to sit on the rug. She wrapped the blanket around both their shoulders and smiled encouragingly. 'Tell me.'

Túathal raised his eyes to hers. 'She couldn't see me,' he whispered. 'She didn't look at me. But she was singing for me. She went up to the edge and looked out and sung of our home. I wanted to touch her, let her know it was me, but…' Sobs racked his body and he covered his face.

'I told you,' Fiadh said, as gently as she could. 'She's a vision. The lighthouse remembers her, but she's not here. Not anymore.'

Túathal rubbed his teary face against the shoulder of his seal pelt. 'Then where is she now, Fiadh?'

Fiadh shook her head helplessly. 'I don't know. I don't know anything. I thought the lighthouse was giving me answers, but it's not. I shouldn't have stayed to try and unravel the mystery of this magic. I should've just left things alone.'

'I wouldn't have met you.'

'And you'd be safer for it! I'm dangerous, Túathal.'

Túathal touched her cheek and gently guided her to look at him. 'You didn't hurt me at all, Fiadh. You didn't even touch me. I sang, you calmed down. Then, after my mother… later, I carried you down.'

Fiadh raised her eyebrows. 'You *carried* the wolf? And it didn't savage you? It just… *slept?*'

He shrugged and managed a smile. 'You're not so dangerous.'

Fiadh looked down at her hands, folded in her lap. Túathal's head drooped onto her knee and she jumped in surprise. He'd stretched out on his back under the blanket. He looked up into her startled face, his own creased pensively.

'Why did my mother stay here if it made her sad?'

Fiadh gave him a small, sympathetic smile, her eyes trailing over the silver curls spilling across her lap. She ran her hand through his glossy hair. Hair that tumbled over her crossed legs like gentle waves and smelled of sea foam.

'Well,' she began, still absentmindedly stroking his hair. 'She didn't have her pelt. So she couldn't…'

'Yes, that's right.' Túathal's face twisted in pain. 'She didn't have her pelt. So she must have lost it, or…'

'Someone must've stolen it,' Fiadh finished, fighting the catch in her throat. Her stomach turned sour, her hand freezing, tangled in Túathal's hair. Remembering her father's hands running over animal pelts as he skinned them.

Her father.

Her heart ached. *Why did you do it? Why did you steal the pelt? Why did you give it to me?*

Everything was my father's fault.

Fiadh blinked. In her memory, Brenna's words rang with all their original vehemence.

Brenna's father. The lighthouse keeper… the lighthouse keeper! *He angered the tide and incited a curse as deep as the ocean itself,* Brenna had said, bitterness and heartache blazing in her words. What could he have done to anger the tide itself? Fiadh felt herself go cold as she traced the threads and saw them drawing together.

He had taken Túathal's mother, a daughter of the ocean. *He* had stolen her pelt and imprisoned her in the belly of his home. The lighthouse. A building designed to guide seafarers safely to shore. And he—

Fiadh covered her mouth, eyes wide.

Brenna.

She glanced down at Túathal. His eyes were closed, chest rising and falling in the rhythm of sleep. His long, watchful night had overtaken him, it seemed. She brushed a lock of hair out of his face. 'Oh, Túathal.'

Carefully, she lowered his head from her knee and down onto the folds of her blanket. She padded silently to the front door and opened it. Looking out, she saw that a fresh snow had fallen while she slept. The air was crisp and heavy with cold, the sky above a brilliant blue, the snow sharp white.

She looked over her shoulder at her sleeping friend, lingering only for a moment. She braced herself against the doorjamb as the wolf's pelt crawled over the rest of her skin.

And then she was running, her four paws drumming a steady beat as she flew through the snow towards the woods.

21

BRENNA'S heavy boots crunched on the new snow. She hitched her knapsack more comfortably on her back. Her shoes and socks were already wet through and her feet felt like blocks of ice. She clicked her tongue. What was the point of finding the wolf if she wasn't able to chase it when she did?

Lowering her eyes to the snow-crusted undergrowth, she searched for tracks. She was no hunter, she reflected with annoyance. She'd spent very little time in the woods growing up, although they were only a couple hundred metres of shrubby grassland from Sjavaba. Her father's work and mother's stories had fostered a greater interest in the sea than the forest. The woods hunched on the border of her world like some sort of blurry wall, hemming her in. The inland settlements and towns beyond hadn't interested her. Not when the ocean spilled out before her, open and vast and full of promises. Not when she felt the tide drag at her knees, as if it felt she was one with it.

The lighthouse and docks and ships that anchored there had been her schoolrooms. She'd learned the inner workings of the lighthouse's mechanism at her father's elbow. Had, at times, been trusted to tinker with it and help with repairs. When her father had spoken to sailors aboard their ships, she'd been allowed to explore the bridge. She would run to the prow and lean out over the edge, her hair wind-whipped fire. Peering into the murky green-blue, she'd catch shimmering movement and imagine that her mother's tales were true.

Brenna sometimes remembered the dreams that younger version of herself had cherished. Fuzzy plans of smuggling her mother onto a ship and sailing them away to find the islands her mother had whispered of. Maybe Idunn's dark eyes would've softened with a hopeful light. Maybe she would've smiled.

Fine dreams. But only dreams.

When the time had come, Idunn had left without her daughter.

And here I am again, Brenna thought. She shook her head to clear it. All roads of thought here – in Sjavaba and her whole hemmed-in world – led back to the same over-trodden paths, the same painful, sour memories. And now, with the once-friendly ocean raging with her father's curse, there was only one way out.

Which brought her to her current task and how hopelessly inept she was at woodcraft.

'Come on, wolf,' she muttered, noting the angle of the sun as it tipped down to the west. 'I'm losing daylight.'

Sighing, she shrugged her knapsack off her back, kneeling to rummage for her water flask. She uncapped it and raised it to her lips. Mid-swig, she heard a sound behind her. Soft and careful. A muted crunch as something passed lightly over the snow.

Heart hammering, Brenna recapped her flask with trembling fingers. She tried to keep her movements slow, fighting the screaming temptation to spin around and face whatever had snuck up behind her. She gritted her teeth and slowly stood up, turned her head.

'Fiadh!'

The wiry girl was rising from a crouch, hands and feet wet with snow. She brushed her hair back from her flushed face, streaking it with mud.

'Sorry, Brenna. I didn't mean to sneak up on you.'

Brenna could've thrown her water flask at the other girl's head. 'Well, I'm glad you're *sorry!*' she exclaimed, still shaking. Dropping her flask, she marched to Fiadh. The pale girl shrank back.

Brenna pulled her into a hug that surprised them both.

'Brenna?'

But she didn't let go. She held Fiadh close, feeling the sharp contours of the other girl's frame. Her white fur coat was rich and warm under Brenna's coarse hands.

It was absurd. Nonsensical. The girl was practically a stranger, but Brenna didn't want to let her go. Didn't want to lose her again. Why had she left in the first place? Why had she run without saying goodbye, without looking back—

Why, Mamma?

Brenna released Fiadh abruptly and stepped away from her.

'It's good you're all right,' she stammered in her confusion. 'You should really stop coming and going without warning.' Her words sounded harsher than she meant them to, but Fiadh didn't seem hurt. Her head was tilted slightly to the side, her expression painfully pitying. As if she could guess some of what Brenna was feeling. As if she knew Brenna, far better than Brenna knew her. An uncomfortable thought. Yet somehow, Brenna realised, she would give the promised horse and cart for it to be true.

'Still hunting your wolf?' Fiadh clasped her hands behind her back and moved to Brenna's side. Brenna took the unspoken cue and hefted her knapsack onto her back, as they started walking. Brenna watched her companion sidelong.

'Yes. Still hunting the wretched thing.'

'Ouch.'

'You haven't seen it?'

Fiadh gave the slimmest hesitation before replying, a little too brightly, 'No. Never laid eyes on it.'

Brenna grunted. 'That's good, in a way.'

Fiadh fell silent again. Brenna kept her eyes downcast, looking for prints she doubted she'd notice even if they were there.

'Brenna,' Fiadh said, after a few moments walking together in silence. 'Last time we talked, you told me about your father.' Brenna pursed her lips. 'Your mother, though… what was she like?' She reached tentatively out and tweaked a lock of Brenna's hair. 'Did you get this from her?'

Brenna could've laughed. 'No. I look nothing like her.'

'Oh?'

'She… was different to any other person I've ever met. She was a foreigner, Father said. I've seen plenty of foreigners, but no one else like her.' She paused. Fiadh kept watching her, waiting for her to go on. 'I always thought she was the prettiest woman I'd ever seen,' she admitted at last. Absently, she turned her face in the direction of the sea, closing her eyes and breathing in through her nose. 'I loved her very much.'

'Loved?'

'It's hard to love someone after they abandon you.' Brenna turned her face away. It wasn't true – not *always* true. The bitterness was real. The ache in her chest whenever she remembered her mother's voice, her faraway eyes, was real. Her anger at having to find out the way she had that her mother had left her sleeping in their bed and gone into the night was so *real*.

But despite it all, she still loved her.

Fiadh took Brenna's hand. Brenna looked down at them. Wiry, milk-pale fingers with ragged nails clasped her work-worn, freckled hand. She raised her eyes, searching Fiadh's face.

'My mother's name was Elowyn,' Fiadh said. Warm and gentle and intimate. 'One time my father called her "princess", and for a year I believed he'd whisked her away from a palace somewhere to live as his bride in the woods.'

'She looked so small next to my father,' Brenna murmured. 'She cowered when he spoke to her. She wouldn't meet his eyes.'

'She only seemed to know the words to one song. So she just hummed the rest of the time.' Fiadh's lips curled into a fond smile.

'She sang all the time! Her voice made my heart yearn, like I'd lost something half-forgotten.'

'I carry a lock of her hair. She had yellow hair. Yellow as butter.'

Brenna ran a hand unconsciously through her red mane. 'My mother's hair was long and smooth. Silver and fawn.' The other girl nodded, as if she'd known already. Brenna frowned. Fiadh hadn't been surprised by any of what she'd told her, as though she'd known all of it before Brenna had even opened her mouth. 'Who are you?'

Fiadh's hand tightened in hers. 'Fiadh—'

'No, I mean it.'

'—daughter of Sion and Elowyn—'

'Stop.' Brenna squeezed Fiadh's fingers tightly. 'Who *are* you? Why do you know so much about me?'

Fiadh ran a hand over her pursed lips, avoiding Brenna's eyes. Finally, she said, 'I'm trying to put the pieces together.' She clasped Brenna's hands in both of her own. They were cold and dirty, but Brenna didn't pull away. Those hands had reached for hers when everyone else she'd known had recoiled from her. She held her breath, waiting.

'I'm a friend, if you'll let me be. I want to help you.'

'Help me?' Brenna repeated, a catch in her voice. 'How? Are you any good at tracking?'

'You really need to find this wolf?'

'If I do, I'll be able to get out of here.'

'Away from your father's shadow?'

Brenna pulled her hand gently free. 'Yes.'

Pausing, Fiadh looked down at her feet, tinged purple under the streaks of dirt. Perhaps a trick of the shifting shadows, perhaps betraying she was colder than she seemed. 'I can't help you hunt the wolf,' she said finally. 'But maybe… maybe there's another way.' She touched Brenna's hand. 'Stay safe. I'll find you again.'

Fiadh made to slip away, but Brenna caught her arm. 'No,' she protested, eyes hard. 'Don't keep doing that!'

Fiadh blinked, before her expression softened. She smiled gently. 'If you need to find me, Brenna, I'll be at the lighthouse.' She freed herself and strode away. Brenna lurched to follow, but soon lost her among the grey and black trees. Opened her mouth to shout after her, but let the call die on her tongue. Sighed, her shoulders sagging.

'At the lighthouse…' Brenna repeated, into the silence. 'You may as well be at the bottom of the sea.'

22

TÚATHAL raised himself from the slate floor. A shiver ran through him. He looked around but saw no sign of Fiadh. The open door creaked on its hinges. Closing his eyes, he listened. The roar of the tide was louder outside, but he could not only hear it. He could *feel* it. Thrumming inside him. Beating in time with his heart.

He stood up and walked out the door, feet sinking into the snow so that he waded through it, like walking through the shallows. As he approached the lip of the cliff that loomed over the sacred beach, he saw his people, clustered loosely along the shore. They rippled with movement, lifting their heads and bodies from the sand, all shifting to look out towards the horizon. A speckled brown woman slowly rose to her feet. She opened her mouth and sang a deep melody. The brides repeated her lilting notes. The foam whispered its call. The waves beckoned them home.

All throughout the gathering, the women stood, singing in response to the retreating tide. The grooms watched, rumbling their part low in their chests. Túathal felt the song reverberate in his own throat, even as he stood above the rest, on the precipice.

He caught sight of Dula as her feet struck through the frothing water. She raised her hands to her spotted hood, flipped it over her face, and dived into the breakers. A flash of tail. Then she was gone, along with her sisters, the brides of the season.

Túathal heard footfalls behind him.

'What's happening?' Fiadh whispered. She glanced at him and

118

then at the grooms below, scattered on the black sands. 'Where are Dula and the other brides?'

Túathal let the note trail away on his lips, leaving his brothers to carry the song to its completion. 'They left. The tide called them home.'

'To your islands?'

'Yes.'

'Why aren't the grooms leaving too?'

'We'll be called, in time.'

'When?'

Túathal turned to look at her. Fiadh. His moon. She'd called him to follow and uncover the answers he so desperately wanted. They'd pulled back a veil last night, her hand guiding his. Part of his mother's story had been brought into the light. But there were yet more questions and he knew – he felt so certain – he wouldn't discover the truth without her.

He found her hand and held it tightly in his. 'Too soon.'

⌘

Fiadh felt his grip tighten as he stepped away, drawing her to the lip of the cliff, as he himself was drawn.

'Wait, Túathal…'

Maybe he couldn't hear her over the low roar of the tide, over whatever pull it had on him. He didn't wait. He stepped recklessly over the edge, seeking a path down to his brothers on the shore.

Fiadh glanced at the sky, bit her lip, and followed.

In the gathering twilight, she dropped to the black sands behind Túathal. The sweeping crescent of the shore glowed with dim star-like sparks. She cast her eyes around at the grooms resting on the beach, who stared as one out to the sea, transfixed. Their song still hung in the air. Then she looked up. The sky was bruising into night.

'I shouldn't be here, Túathal,' she breathed. She hadn't meant for the others to hear, but her words seemed to awaken those nearest from the spell of the brides' departure. She sucked her lip, crossed her arms self-consciously over her chest.

Túathal didn't seem to hear her. He strode to where the foam hissed on the sand. Lurched into the water, striving forward until he was up to his waist in the surf. Knelt and plunged his hands and face below the surface. Fiadh watched from the high tide line as he resurfaced, his glossy hair running over the contours of his face, slicked down the back of his neck. His hands skimmed over the water and he tilted his chin up to look at the sky. Vast and open and limitless. A far cry from the oppressively small world of the lighthouse's walls.

Fiadh stepped back. She would leave him to grieve. To mourn with the tide for that other bride.

As she turned away, a dark shape collided with her shoulder, spinning her around. Quillen splashed into the water and embraced Túathal.

'Brother! Where have you been?' Quillen exclaimed. He framed his friend's cheeks, searching his face. His hands fell to Túathal's shoulders and he checked him over.

'Quillen.' Túathal spoke softly, sounding heart-weary. 'Nowhere I did not intend to be.'

Turning, Quillen looked at Fiadh, where she hovered on the shore. She caught her breath. There was hostility in the lines of his expression. 'The pelt-stealer stole you too,' he hissed.

Fiadh shook her head, clutching her hands to her chest. She glanced at Túathal, expecting him to protest, to explain, but his eyes were glazed and downcast. Her gaze strayed to the sky, to the deep grey that was flooding out the last red and umber streaks of the fading sun. She took another step back. 'I can't be here—'

'No.' Túathal raised his head. Brushed away Quillen's protective hands and rose up out of the water to meet her. Fiadh's heart chilled. His face – his laughing, open, tender face – was hard, his eyes cold. 'You need to stay.' His voice, too, was harsh.

'Túathal,' she whispered urgently, glancing at the nearby men.

They were staring, expressions oddly blank, as if an enchantment hung over them. Their dark eyes were haunting. A shiver ran through her. 'Túathal, I have to get out of here before the wolf wakes!'

'I can calm it.'

'What if that was by chance? I can't risk that!' She shook her head decisively and spun around to leave, but Túathal's hand closed on her wrist. She gasped. His grip was icy. Tight.

'Túathal!' Her voice was high with fear. Fear of the wolf and, for the first time, fear of him.

'Who stole my mother's pelt, Fiadh?'

Pressing her lips together, she looked up into his face. She felt herself shaking. Gooseflesh rose over her arms, fine hairs bristling. Her senses began to sharpen. She could hear the slap-hiss of the lapping waves, the breathing of each of the gathered selkie grooms. The subtle stirring of sand in the wind. Túathal's scent was all about her, overpowering every other, except for the ever-present musk of the wolf. Even so, her mind started to cloud, to wander…

Fiadh bit her lip until she tasted blood. Blinked furiously, forcing herself to focus on Túathal's sharp face. She could see, could *feel*, his anger. It seethed behind his eyes.

'It was a human, Fiadh. It had to be.' He didn't raise his voice.

'Túathal—'

'They hurt my mother, Fiadh. Who stole her pelt?'

Could she calm his anger? *Should* she try to still the turbulent rage brewing inside him? And what would he do if he knew the extent of his mother's torment? If he had even an inkling that her captor had fathered her second child, a daughter, a girl with flaming hair and a bitter mouth?

No. Túathal couldn't know. Not now. His anger was too raw.

Fiadh reached up and touched his cheek, finding it wet with salt water. 'He's dead, Túathal. The man who hurt your mother. He's dead. He can't hurt her anymore, and… you can't hurt him.' His grip tightened on her wrist. She winced, shuddering as the wolf stirred. 'Please—'

'How can we trust anything you say?' Quillen demanded, coming up behind them. '*Pelt-stealer!*'

That broke the spell transfixing the rest. Whispering and hissing broke out all around her. Movement. Shadows in the dark.

The dark!

'Túathal!'

Quillen rested a hand on Túathal's shoulder, his face blurring before Fiadh's eyes. She let out a shuddering cry and doubled over. 'What's wrong with her?' Quillen muttered in disgust, too loudly for her sensitive ears.

'She can't control her second skin. It is predator instinct alone.'

'Túathal! I know you're angry, but please, don't let me change out here!'

'The humans' settlement,' Túathal said. 'It's just on the other side of the outcrop.'

Quillen's voice was snide. 'She's just one creature.'

'I don't want to hurt anyone!' Fiadh screamed. She beat at Túathal's chest. Thrashed in his unwavering hold. Her eyes wide with a horrible, shrieking terror. 'Don't do this! Don't use me like some – some *monster!* I don't want to be its vessel! I've taken advantage of it, over and over and over and I hate – I *hate* – that I can't resist it anymore! I hate that I've hurt people! Túathal!' She broke off, coughing with wet sobs. 'Túathal—'

'*LET ME GO!*'

The shriek rent the air. Fiadh's throat ripped red-raw with the force of it. Her ears rang with the sound of it. Túathal's hand spasmed and she fell heavily onto the sands, as Túathal reeled and collapsed, eyes staring at a point behind Fiadh. Still fighting for a few more seconds of lucidity, Fiadh twisted around to follow the line of his gaze.

The grooms were gone. The night was thick and dark. Lit for a faltering heartbeat by a great, white light. And in the middle of the beach, a woman tore free from a man's choking embrace. She fell forward, long hair streaming behind her like a pennant blown in the wind. The man, red curls sparking in the irregular flash of the great light, staggered backwards. In one large hand he clasped a crumpled mass of fur. A lantern swung, squealing, from the other, a pinprick of stuttering light.

The man's chest heaved. He threw the pelt to the ground and cracked the lantern open with his bare hands. A stream of oil ran down his fingers, hands, forearms. Spattered onto the folds of the pelt. The flame sputtered, recoiling from the violence it was about to commit.

Too late.

He flung the broken lantern down with a roar that reverberated in Fiadh's ribs. The oil caught. The pelt burst into leaping tongues of fire. The woman's screams pierced Fiadh to her core.

Túathal's mother staggered to her feet. The thin white dress whipped about her knees, her thighs. Her hair streamed wildly around her, tangling and writhing with the winds. The white beam of the lighthouse's heartbeat flashed across the scene, illuminating the terrible anguish of her expression.

She leapt into the water. The cold convulsed her. She thrashed in the shallows. The breakers swamped her. She resurfaced, coughing, crying. The man shouted after her, tried to follow. The flames turned on him. Sparks caught on his sleeve, in his hair. He raced after her.

But by the time he plunged into the foam, she was gone. And the surging ocean waters drowned out his roars with theirs.

23

THE vision melted into the dusk of the present. Túathal sensed Quillen beside him, but his friend's worried words were far away. The blood in his ears pounded in time with the rapid rise and fall of his chest. He was trembling all over. Shivering in the wake of the horror he had witnessed. The lighthouse's memory, clear and sharp and raw.

His mother. The woman who'd appeared so small and faded in the lighthouse. She'd been defiant and spirited at the last, just like Túathal's father had always described her.

But it hadn't been enough.

He heard screaming, sobbing, far off. With a jolt, he realised they were his own cries. His cries for his mother. Lost so long ago. Swallowed up by the tide. A sudden enemy made by the burning of her pelt.

The world juddered back into focus, sounds rushing in all at once. Quillen, jostling him by the shoulder, was shouting at him to move, to look at him, to do *something!* The other grooms were calling to one another to retreat to the sea. For a baffled second, Túathal thought they must've seen the vision too. Was the man of fire somehow still ablaze on the shore? He raised his head.

The wolf glowed white on the glitter-black sand. Red mouth open. Teeth gleaming. A gravelly snarl rumbled in its throat. It snapped, lunging at the closest grooms. They yelped and scattered.

'Fiadh…' he rasped, barely a breath. Fumbled for Quillen's arm, turned to look into his wide-eyed face. 'Quillen, sing with me! We have to calm her.'

Quillen glanced at him but shook his head. 'We don't need to.' He hauled Túathal up and started dragging him backwards into the swell of the tide.

The foam washed over his feet. He stared down at them, sinking into the very tide that had drowned his mother. Jerked his head up again to see the wolf deserted on the sands, hemmed in by high walls and the savage black sea.

Fiadh was trapped. Imprisoned in a pelt she couldn't escape. Alone. And he'd wanted to hold her there. *Use* her.

Túathal felt sick.

He twisted free from Quillen's grasp. His friend grunted in exasperation, but he was already leaping forward, scrambling to the wolf's side. He had to get to her. Had to calm her. Protect her. Free her. Bring her home.

It's too late. She's gone.

Not yet!

His sudden dash startled the wolf. Ears pressed back on its head, it snarled. He opened his mouth to sing, but his tongue tripped over the words, the melody faltering in his raw throat.

The wolf turned and ran.

Túathal skidded in the sand. Fell. Picked himself up, just in time to see the wolf spring for the crevice in the cliff face and vanish into the cave.

'Túathal!' Quillen caught him before he could give chase. 'Túathal, leave it!' He held him fast. Took Túathal's face in his hands. Forced him to meet his eyes. 'A pelt-stealer like her deserves not your pity. Come! Swim with your brothers. Sing with us.'

'No, Quillen.' Túathal clutched a fistful of Quillen's black-brown pelt. Holding onto him but holding him at a distance. 'No. She asked for my help and I betrayed her. She's losing herself. She's lost and scared and I—' He let go of Quillen and broke away. 'I need to make it right.'

He ran. His body felt heavy and clumsy on the land. When he swam with his brothers in the depths, in his home seas, he was light and agile, almost elegant. Yet now, he tripped. Caught himself on the coarse rock of the cliff. Ducked into the tunnel. It was dark, only a faint gleam of silvery light touching the wet cave walls. Even so, his eyes were sharp. Quillen's protests died behind him.

The cave echoed with the *lap-lap-lap* of water on its walls, the inconstant dripping of water in the shallows. His feet splashed loudly in the puddles, then into the swell of the tide as he bolted out into the open again. Stars winked slowly into the night sky above. A chill wind sang through the crevices in the cliff.

Túathal ran down into the tide, around the jagged teeth of the outcrop, up the beach again. Up a wreckage of sodden wood that might once have formed some sort of platform jutting over the water. Stopped at the top, breathing hard. Looked up.

He'd only ever seen Sjavaba from a distance, poking his whiskered face above the waves to peer at the human settlement. It hadn't seemed anything special to him. A grey smudge on the black, white, and dead-green of the winter landscape. Or a cluster of fallen starlight on the night-time coast. From where he now stood, the ruins smothered any lamplight. And Fiadh – the monstrous city had swallowed her up. He was sure of it.

Túathal hesitated to approach the looming darkness. Ran his hands through his hair. Dithered agitatedly, shifting his weight from one foot to the other and back. Every second, he was keenly aware, Fiadh ran further and further into the maze of buildings. What might she do to the people she encountered?

The wolf was a predator. Lashing out on instinct alone. Without his song to calm her – a selkie calling out to a long-lost remnant of his kin – what would she do?

Her hands were gentle and kind. Her voice empathetic, earnest.

He remembered her urgency that morning, her desperation to know whether she'd harmed him. She was so afraid of her pelt. So afraid that the wolf would hurt those close to her. How could he have even for a moment dreamed of unleashing that savagery, when its vessel feared and resented it so?

He balled his hands into fists, fingernails digging into the soft flesh of his palms. And still he couldn't make the plunge. Still couldn't leap into the congealed shadows. Humans beyond count dwelled behind those ruined walls. He had reason enough to be wary, reason enough to fear them.

Beware. You are in dangerous waters.

That had never stopped him before.

Túathal lurched forward, clawing at caution to throw it aside. But it clung to him like a third skin. Crawled over him. Whispered nasty fears in his ear as he darted gracelessly through the ruins.

What would happen if he ran into the humans that inhabited the city? He knew it all too well. They'd steal his pelt, and his joy and freedom with it. Imprison him. Cut him off from the sea and the sky. Like they'd done to his mother, so she'd wept instead of laughed, floated wraithlike instead of danced.

Humans had inhabited the earliest stories of his childhood, like phantom echoes of his own people. They were mysterious but persistent creatures. Tied to the land by their forms, but relentless in their pursuit of liberty – learning to swim despite their land-built frames, building sea vessels to travel pathways that ought to have been closed to them. Freedom and the pursuit of it seemed so integral to their people that tales of pelt-stealers had grated against his sensibilities.

Túathal called Fiadh's name as he ran. He stopped every few minutes, turning on the spot, peering under obstructions. Straining his eyes for a glimpse of white fur. The ruins melted behind him, the streets becoming clearer. Dirty, but no longer covered in tumbled debris. Lamplight winked in windows and his fear mounted, stifling his breath.

The pride he'd always known in his people, in their dual forms… the world was richer to him because he could experience it with two bodies. Could dance and swim, sing and croon, dream with eyes open and slumber dreamless. He'd never questioned that he belonged to both the seal and the human. But he was not human. He didn't belong here. He was trespassing.

Running like a fugitive in a stolen skin.

A scream – shrill, short – pierced the rhythm of his heart and feet. He stopped, turning wildly. A door creaked open down the street. He ducked into the shelter of shadows, but even as he darted towards the sound, lights flared behind clouded glass and spilled from opened doors. People peered out. Stepped out. Túathal gritted his teeth and kept running, forcing himself not to turn and look at the people looming into view as silhouettes in flickering light.

Fiadh.

Sounds of a commotion. Shouts and cries. Names called out. Feet stomping, crunching, sliding.

Fiadh.

A snarl, low and aggressively afraid. A howl. A blunt *whack*. A yelp. A bruised whimper—

'Fiadh!'

Túathal hurtled around a corner. He found himself in a broad street lined with narrow buildings. A crowd had gathered at the foot of uneven steps. A young man with jet-black hair stood at the top of the stairs, gripping the railing tightly, staring into the throng. Túathal moved closer.

And there she was. He glimpsed her through the legs and arms and shifting bodies hemming her in with fear, with anger.

His fear ebbed. His anger swelled.

Without a second thought, he shoved his way through the mob of people. He was deaf to their grunts of surprise, deaf to their protests. He pushed aside a man holding a broom at the ready like a club. The man shoved him back and he fell forward into the middle of the circle. Right in front of the wolf. It growled, but weakly. Ears flat on its skull, it cowered by the steps.

'Fiadh,' he breathed, unafraid. How could he fear her? He crawled towards her. Held out the back of his hand to her. 'It's me, Fiadh. It's Túathal.'

The wolf whined, still scared. He opened his mouth to say he was sorry. To say he hated what he'd said to her, how he'd trapped her when she'd tried to flee. To renounce whoever he'd been, whatever anger and pain had caused him to become. But the wolf's eyes glowed amber. He swallowed those words. He'd save them until he could speak them to Fiadh, the true Fiadh. Instead, he opened his mouth to sing.

'Oi!'

Túathal started and looked over his shoulder. It was the man with the broom. Túathal remembered the whack he'd heard as he'd sprinted to Fiadh's side. His blood ran cold. This man had struck her!

'What are you doing?'

Túathal bared his teeth and flung out an arm to shield the wolf.

'Who are you?' hissed another voice from the crowd.

'*What* are you?'

'Where did you come from?'

Túathal's eyes darted back and forth between the hecklers. Fiadh snarled. He reached out a hand to calm her and the wolf struck. Its teeth clamped on his wrist. Sank into his flesh. Blood beaded on his skin, stained its teeth.

Túathal cried out. The crowd seethed, the man with the broom swinging it down to crack cruelly on the wolf's head. The wolf tore loose. Túathal shouted for it to stop, to stay, but the crowd blocked off its escape. It skittered back, scrambled up the stairs. The young man at the top yelped and jumped onto the rail, almost toppling backwards. The wolf's claws clattered on the steps. It leapt from the landing down into the street beyond the mob. Darted away. Winked out of sight amidst the night shadows and pale-yellow lamplight scattered on the cobbles.

Túathal jumped up but reeled and fell back. Someone in the crowd caught him as he swooned. He looked blearily down at his bloody wrist. Dark red drops, almost black in the dim lamplight, spattered the churned snow at his feet. He clamped his other hand over the wound, vainly trying to staunch the flow.

There wasn't time for this.

Fiadh…

'Hey, will you all just – oof! Let me *through!* Oh, that looks nasty.' The young man had hopped down from the top of the stairs. Took Túathal's arm, fingers cool on his skin. He tried to push the young man aside, but he barely glanced up from inspecting the wound. 'Yes, sure thing. I'd love to let you to waltz off after the wolf that bit you. My pleasure, sane sir.' He was already steering Túathal towards the steps.

'She's getting away!'

'Mmhm?'

'Let me—'

The young man swung Túathal's good arm over his shoulder and hauled him up the steps to the narrow, dark-fronted building. 'Hustle on, folks. Nothing to gawk at anymore – though someone should get about informing the Council. And Einar! What the hell do you think you were doing? If that was the feywalker, *you'd* be cursed for striking it, you bloody idiot.'

Without waiting for an answer, he shouldered the door open and dragged Túathal across the threshold. As soon as they were alone, his demeanour changed. Throwing a look over his shoulder, he hustled Túathal behind tall wood-and-paper folding screens and lowered him to sit on a cot. Stepped away, stopped. Glanced at Túathal, eyes flicking up and down his body. Held out his palm – *stay* – and ducked around the screen.

'*Afi*, come down! You're going to want to see our patient!'

Túathal's body felt heavy, his head light. He tried to focus. To force his body to move. Every second, Fiadh was further away. Who would she run into next? Would they be stronger? More afraid? More violent?

Move…

His head ached from crying through the night. Wincing, he clamped his hand tighter over the wolf's bite marks to stifle the lancing pain. His heart still hammered from his wild pursuit.

Move!

'What is all th-this racket about, Bo?' an elderly voice demanded from the other side of the screens.

'See for yourself.'

'For heaven's *sake* – oh!'

Túathal stood, fighting a wave of dizziness. The old man's grey hair fell loose to his shoulders, his russet eyes wide with surprise. Túathal frowned. There was recognition in that weathered face.

'Idunn…' the old man breathed.

'That's my mother's name,' he said groggily. 'Why?'

Bo glanced between them. 'Wasn't Idunn…'

His grandfather crossed to Túathal. He barely came up to the selkie's shoulder. For a moment, he gaped up at Túathal, before pressing his lips together and forcing a smile that he surely meant to be gentle. It looked more like a grimace scratched onto his creased face. The crinkles gathered at the corners of his eyes deepened – and those *eyes*. They gazed into Túathal, aglow with a depth of intimacy he couldn't reciprocate. His legs shook and he sank back onto the cot.

'Son of the tide and the storm,' the old man whispered in a worn, dry voice. His hand moved as if to stroke the damp fur of Túathal's pelt. Instead, he rested his palm reverently on Túathal's head. 'I am sorry.'

'*Afi*…'

'I knew her heritage. I knew what she was. I knew at least a little of her plight. But I didn't learn it quickly enough. Nor was I… strong enough to aid her.'

Túathal blinked. Swallowed. Tried to say that it didn't matter now, that it was too late, had been too late for years. That what *did* matter was Fiadh. Out in the open. Needing him. And there was still time to aid her.

But he couldn't say it. His lips trembled. Covering his face with his hands, he curled inward, the force of his agony and his grief crippling him.

Because of course it mattered. It would always matter.

24

'FIADH, please. Sit with me.'

Sion patted his thigh, encouraging her to climb into his lap. He smiled, but it didn't sit comfortably on his face. His eyebrows were knitted together and his mouth looked too tight.

He was sitting on the edge of the bed in the single room of the hunter's cabin he'd hired. It'd been a hard winter for them. A hard year. Fiadh still sometimes forgot that her mother, Elowyn, wasn't in the cabin. That she wouldn't find her lining the clothes chest with herbs to discourage moths, salting the meat her husband had caught for them, or helping him mend his tools. That she wouldn't wake up to Elowyn's off-key humming, or come upon her in the wood at the back of the cabin, gathering herbs or sorting nuts. Sometimes, Fiadh almost forgot that her mother, with her messy yellow hair falling loose from its pins, her weak eyes crinkled prematurely from squinting, her hands textured with hard work… Fiadh almost forgot that she lived only in those memories.

Sion never forgot. Fiadh knew that Elowyn's death last summer weighed on his mind every waking moment, buzzed like a hum in his ear he couldn't drown out. She knew because he didn't go hunting anymore. He couldn't rouse himself to do it. Even on those days he did take up his bow or spear – shook them free from their coating of dust and ventured into the woods – he didn't return with game on his shoulders. Did grief make the animals scarce? Did guilt make it hard to shoot straight?

So, they ran out of pelts to sell. Ran out of meat to eat. Ran out of options.

'Come, wild one. We… we don't have long.' His eyes flicked to the door Fiadh had just pulled closed. She sucked her lip and bent to take off her boots. 'No, my cub.' He swiped the corner of his eye with one thumb and dragged in a shaky breath. 'Keep them on.'

'What is it, *Pabbi?*' Fiadh sat beside him on the bed. She'd grown too much in the past four seasons to sit in his lap. 'Are we… are we losing the cabin?'

Sion pulled her close and hugged her. Cupped her face in his hands, stroked her cheek with his thumb, peered into her violet eyes. Her mother's eyes. 'Oh, my cub!' He bowed his head, breathing shakily. Looked up and nodded. 'Yes,' he murmured. 'Yes, we're losing the cabin. But it's worse than that. Can you imagine it? I made it even worse than that.'

'It can't be too bad, *Pabbi*,' Fiadh said, putting her hand over his. 'Even without the cabin, we'll be fine. When you and Mamma were young, you lived in the woods. Mamma told me—'

'It won't be *we*, wild one. It'll be you. Just you.'

Fiadh pulled away from him. 'What do you mean?'

Her father dashed at his eyes. 'I'm so sorry I brought it to this. I wanted to get some money. So we could keep the cabin, have food on the table…' His gaze strayed to her thin, faded clothes. Her frayed sleeves. 'So I could clothe my daughter.'

'What happened?'

'The winter was too harsh here. Many of the beasts died or moved off. There wasn't any decent game to hunt, cub. But then, I thought, there's always game on the estate land…'

Fiadh covered her mouth. '*Pabbi!*'

'I know. Fiadh, I know.'

'They saw you?'

'They saw *through* me. When I went to sell the pelts, the buyer sold me out.'

Fiadh tossed a look over her shoulder, almost expecting the lord's men to come bursting through that very moment with a warrant to arrest the poacher. 'What do we do? Why are we still here?' She jumped up from the bed. 'We shouldn't need much. Your bow. Hunting knives. Some nuts.'

'Fiadh.'

'Maybe we should cut your hair first, or you could shave—'

Sion caught her hands and gripped them in his own. Now, his smile was real. Tender and sad, but real. He knelt in front of her, crushing her hands to his lips. His breath sighed warm on her knuckles as he spoke.

'There's no need, my darling. I'm not running from the wrong I have done – I just needed to tell you first. Prepare you.'

Fiadh felt tears prickle at her eyes. Her father brushed them away.

'I don't think I'll ever be prepared.' She fought the words out of her trembling lips. 'We just lost Mamma. I can't lose you too.'

'Oh, wild one. You're not losing me. I'll make amends with the lord. It may take months, or years, but we won't lose each other forever. It's going to be hard, but you're a fine young woodswoman. Your job is to take care of yourself until we meet again.'

Rising, he moved to the clothes chest at the foot of the bed, while Fiadh swiped at her tears. He flung the lid open and rummaged through the clothes, upsetting a couple of moths. Something white gleamed underneath the mound of faded fabrics. Her father straightened and shook out the heavy, rich fur.

'I was driven to poaching before, several years ago,' he said. 'That time, I didn't find mere game, but I did find this. It's too precious to sell.' Fiadh edged closer, putting her hand out to touch the pelt. Her father swung it around her and draped it over her shoulders. 'I shouldn't have it. When I skinned the poor wolf, I had no idea its pelt contained the power it does. Listen, Fiadh – it will protect you in my stead. Use it sparingly, only when you really need to. Understand?'

The sound of voices and tramping feet, the clink of sword belts, came to them from outside.

Sion kissed his daughter's forehead.

'Stay strong, wild one. Stay safe. We'll find each other again.'

25

CIAT fell, laughing breathlessly, onto the shale. Túathal tried to pull him back into the dance, but he waved his hands away.

'I can't, I can't,' he panted, grinning. 'I'm too old to dance so long!'

'You're too old to dance at all, Pa!' Túathal laughed.

Ciat yanked his son's arm so he crashed down to the shale beside him. Rolling onto his back, Túathal wheezed with joy-drunk laughter.

'It's the night before my son's bridal pilgrimage!' Ciat exclaimed. 'If there were ever a time to dance again, it's now!'

Túathal sighed, long and loud. 'You could join us, Pa. Dance with some young new bride.'

Ciat elbowed his son in the ribs, mouth stretched in a good-natured grin. 'I didn't think I'd raised an eel, Túathal!'

'I just mean you're not so old you couldn't make a woman happy.'

'Ha!'

Ciat leaned back on his elbows and watched their people. Children and elders danced along and in among the bridal generation. Laughing, gambolling, singing. Splashing up to their knees in the wash of the tide. On the cusp between land and sea.

The smile faded a little from Ciat's face. Túathal noticed the change, as well as he did the changes of the tide.

'Pa?'

'I will never be a groom again.'

'I know.'

The older selkie leaned forward, resting his forearms on his knees. His eyes trailed from the dancers to the tide. To the ocean's vast expanse, the bright moonlight playing on the skin of the deep. 'Maybe you'll finally find her.'

'You think so?'

Ciat smiled. 'I'd like to think so.'

Túathal threw his head back. The moon was a shade away from being perfectly round.

'If you find her out there,' Ciat murmured, after a moment's pause, 'tell her… tell her to come home.'

Túathal rested his head on his father's shoulder, like he used to do when he was small. Facing the morrow, and what futures it may or may not bring, made him feel small. Too small and too young for those deep seas.

'Come back to an old, clumsy dancer like you?' he teased, his gentle tone softening the edge off the words.

Ciat ruffled his son's hair. 'Yes. But, you know? If she did come back to me, Túathal, I'd be a much more graceful dancer.' He closed his eyes. 'I'd be young again.'

26

THE sun broke through the heavy clouds that had blotted out the sky for an entire week. The storms had been so wild and so dark that Brenna hadn't been able to tell the days from the nights. Indeed, she'd begun to fear, as the tempest had lashed the lighthouse with all the fury the heavens could muster, that the storm would never end. That it would finally batter the lighthouse until it broke apart and crumbled into the savage sea.

The sunlight, weak and strained though it was, made her eyes water. She burst out of her prison, her island of shelter, and splashed in the yellow pools of it. Let it soak into her skin as she turned her face to the sky. Let it catch in her hair and set it aflame.

For a while, she enjoyed the moment. Enjoyed the light breeze on her skin. Enjoyed the smell of a washed-clean earth. Enjoyed a precious few minutes between fear of what had been and the fear that was brewing, that was tramping up the hill.

Brenna saw the mob at a distance. She backed away, spun around, and bolted back into the lighthouse, slamming the door closed behind her.

'Father!' she shouted. She ran to the tower and started up the stairs. 'Father!' Flinging the door to the lantern room open, she sprang up the last few steps. Her father sat slumped at the edge of the room, stripped down to his sweat-stained shirt, his eyes deeply shadowed. He barely stirred, even when she knelt and shook his shoulder.

'Father, they're coming again.'

He closed his eyes and groaned a curse. 'Impetuous sharks!'

'Yes, yes, I know.'

'I've worked my *arse* off for eight straight days to keep this beacon lit!' he roared. 'No whelp of a Councilman is going to tell me—'

'It's not just the Council, Father. There are a lot of them.'

He slammed his fist on the wall. Brenna jumped and took several hasty steps back as he clambered heavily to his feet. She cringed against the wall while he paced agitatedly back and forth, swearing. He struck out at the window. Cracks spiderwebbed across the glass. Spinning around, he jabbed a finger at her.

'Go!' he barked. 'Go and tell those bloody *lowlifes* that if they want to snuff out this light, they better come up here and do it themselves!' He kicked the lantern platform. 'I've given the best years of my life to this place! If I didn't keep this thing lit and spinning, no one would…' He trailed away, eyes glazed.

For a second, Brenna wanted to hug him. To cling to the only family she had left. They shared a common grief, didn't they? A common loss. If he held out his arms and said sorry for how he'd treated her mother, for how he'd made them both fear the man they should have been able to love — if he assured her that they'd be all right, that they might weather this assault together… perhaps she could've found it in her heart to forgive him.

He didn't. Of course he didn't.

'What are you *weeping* there for?' he bellowed, eyes snapping back into sharp focus. 'Go tell 'em!'

Brenna fled.

⌘

Elder Emil and Elder Johan forced their way past Brenna and marched into the lighthouse, followed by a score of thunder-faced townsfolk. Their eyes raked over her. She cowered back. The apothecary, his silver-streaked hair tied back in a wolf tail, was the last across the threshold, his mouth twisted with distaste. Several of the crowd hung

140

back. She caught sight of a familiar face and slipped over to talk to him.

'What's this all about, Bo?' she whispered.

The boy's face was red and blotchy. His narrow nose was chafed. 'Get away from me!' he spat.

Brenna flinched. 'Bo?'

She looked at the group lingering outside. Saw their bloodshot, grief-stricken eyes. The anger etched in the lines of their faces. 'My father kept the beacon lit all through the storm!' she said. 'How can any damage be his fault?'

Bo wiped his nose on his sleeve. 'The *storm* is his fault.'

'We know!' Elder Emil's daughter choked, grief and fury staining her cheeks. Shot a look at Brenna that made her recoil. Swiped her eyes with her fingers, the heels of her hands, her wrists, vainly trying to quell her tears. 'We know…'

Bo regarded the widow before turning his blunt gaze to Brenna. '*Afi* told us,' he said, as if revealing a dire secret she'd withheld. 'Your father cursed the sea.'

Brenna shook her head. 'That's ridiculous.'

'The tide waged its vengeance on all of us, for what *he* did.'

'Don't be stupid.'

'The Council's made their judgement.'

Brenna frowned. Shook her head. 'No. No, that's stupid.' A crash behind her. Shouting from inside. And still she was shaking her head, because it wasn't true. It couldn't be real.

She caught Bo's sleeve. He jerked his arm, but she clung to him, shook him, tried to pull him with her. 'Stop them,' she said, though it couldn't be happening. How could it be happening? 'Bo, help me! Stop them!'

He yanked his arm free, sending her reeling, almost falling in the mud. She gaped at him, as he set his chin. Turned his back. Stalked away. And she backed away from him, from them. Twirled on her heel. Sprinted inside.

Bang! The door on the wall. Firewood scattered from the hearth, strewn across the floor. Her feet slipped on a floor slick with oil. Shadows moved, efficient in their vandalism. Clang of pots. Clash of jars breaking.

Sprinting past them. Sprinting up the stairs. Breath chafing her throat. Up and up. Blood thundering in her ears, not loud enough to drown the shouts. The clamour of fighting.

'Father? Father! *FATHER!*

Shattering glass. Shouts and roars, a beast unleashed.

She leapt into the lantern room.

Men crowded at the rail. Staring into the abyss, the yawning monster's mouth. Elder Johan breathing hard. A welt blossoming on his cheekbone. Elder Emil, sword drawn. Red-tipped. Shielded from her by wide-eyed wraiths.

'Father?'

Elder Emil stated, matter-of-fact, 'One more corpse to pollute the beach, then.'

27

TÚATHAL touched the linen strip bound tightly around his wrist. The cloth was coarse and smelled of strange herbs.

'Thank you,' he murmured, stroking the binding curiously.

Yuel sighed and leaned back on his stool. Prising the round spectacles off his nose, he rubbed his weary eyes. 'It's the least I can do for Idunn's son.'

'How did you know my mother?'

Yuel's mouth tweaked, as if he were on the verge of answering. On the verge of sharing a snippet of the mother Túathal had lost so long ago. But he pursed his lips and shook his head.

'It doesn't matter, child.'

He regarded Túathal with an intensity that began to make him feel uncomfortable. Suddenly, Yuel lurched forward. Túathal started, as the old apothecary clutched his arm, fixing him with a stern, pleading gaze.

'Don't hold it against Sjavaba, child,' he whispered in hoarse, earnest voice.

'What?'

'We didn't know what that man had done. He kept her secret from us. Secret for a time, until… until it could be hidden no longer. Even then, I couldn't know what it meant.'

Túathal's skin crawled. He tried to free his hands, but Yuel's fingernails dug into his palms.

'We killed him for his crimes, child. So I beg you. Son of the tide,

143

hold it against us no longer!'

'I don't. I did, but I—'

'Why does the tide still punish us?'

Túathal shook his head helplessly. 'I don't know what you're talking about.'

Yuel stared into Túathal's face, beseeching. Searching. An expression of doubt flickered over his face, his features slackening. Abruptly, he released Túathal, pushing back from the cot. He stood and shuffled past the screen without a backward glance.

A moment later, Bo edged in, looking over his shoulder with a frown nestled on his brows. 'What's up with my grandfather, Silver?' he asked. 'What did you say?'

Túathal swung his legs off the cot. 'I don't know, but I need to go.'

'Oh, for the love of… what's possessing you?' Bo demanded. He flourished a hand at the door. 'It's dark, there's a feywalker wolf-thing out there somewhere – and, to be honest, you're a wreck right now.'

'I don't care. I have to find her. To help her.'

Bo placed his hands on his hips, incredulous. 'The wolf? You're still on about that?'

'The wolf, yes.' Túathal stood up and took a step. Bo stood in his way. Túathal tried to sidestep him, but Bo threw out an arm.

'*Why?*

'She's my friend.'

'Friend? It's an animal, Silver. Or worse, a feywalker. So they say.'

Túathal laughed bitterly, hating the sound of it. He spread his arms. His fur garment swathed him in its loose, mottled folds. 'And what do you think I am? She's like me. We dance up and down the shore, one moment on the sands, the next in the water. One day human, the next a beast! Your grandfather knows.'

'So it *is* a feywalker?'

'No. Maybe, but she's not supposed to be. She needs my help!'

'It's not here to punish Brenna?'

Túathal tossed his hands in the air. 'I have no idea who that is! Fiadh has nothing to do with anyone. The only thing controlling her is the wolf, the wolf side of her. It's taking her over. And I was meant to help her, but I didn't. I made it worse.' He pushed Bo aside. 'I need to find her before she hurts anyone else.'

Túathal reached the door.

'Silver.'

He stopped, hand poised on the knob. Looked over his shoulder. Bo held his gaze for a moment, then sighed.

'Give me a second.'

Túathal watched as the other man strode to the back of the shop. Leaning bodily over the counter, he whisked a coat from a high stool and came back. 'Wear this over that fur thing,' he said.

Túathal took the coat. Leather, lined with fleece.

'Animal skins?'

'Not the type that'll change you into something else, I promise. Turn the collar up and keep your head down so you don't attract attention. You look strange, even in Sjavaba.'

Bo opened the door.

Túathal looked beyond, out into the darkness, and flashed him a grin. He let a taut smile tweak his lip.

'Good luck.'

28

THERE was something strange in the air — some pressure, or strain. Despite the aching weariness in her legs, it kept Brenna from returning home. When the sky bruised purple with evening, she dug a hollow beside a tight copse of trees and lit a small fire. Ate her dinner in silence, straining with every sense to understand the feeling of taut anticipation. Darkness crouched around the feeble light of her flames. An expectant darkness. She could feel it, whistling in the bare branches and snapping in the fire. Could hear, on the very cusp of perception, a call.

Brenna lurched abruptly into action. She opened the glass globe of her lantern and drew a stick from the fire. Careful not to let the flame licking along its length blow out, she lit the wick of her lantern and stood. Now, the anticipation in the air was thrumming. Her chest was tight with it.

There was no time. She couldn't say why she felt that. How she knew. She trembled with the certainty of it.

Knuckles white on the wire handle of her lantern, she thrust the orange light before her. Stabbed the darkness with its guttering glow. And followed it, making her way through the wood.

Knowing, untainted by doubt, that she was going where she needed to go.

29

THE night hummed with noise. Distant chanting or singing, Túathal thought at first, as he hesitated on the bottom step of the apothecary's store. But when he stepped onto the cobbles and followed the noise further up the street, he realised he was wrong.

The apothecary's street opened onto a courtyard, the largest open space he'd yet seen in the town. It glowed with light – the light of torches and lanterns held aloft. For, despite the late hour, the courtyard hosted a crowd of people.

They weren't singing, as he'd expected. They weren't dancing. They hadn't risen in the middle of the night, overcome with the beauty of the stars and the snow. Hadn't gathered in the darkness, unable to contain their joy until the dawn.

No. They were angry. They were afraid. They shouted and argued on the sweeping steps of a grand building, which crouched on the other side of the courtyard, its doors flung wide. A group of twelve older people stood apart from the rest, looking down on them from the steps. Men in grey clothing, trimmings of bronze flashing in the torchlight, held the crowd back.

Túathal edged along the border of the courtyard, skirting the fifty or more people quarrelling at the steps. They didn't spare him a glance. Still, he drew Bo's coat closer over his bulky fur and hunched his shoulders.

'Why wasn't something done about the keeper's brat before?' a voice shouted above the clamour.

'We're still plagued with storms, with the wrath of the sea!'

'And now this wolf – this *feywalker* – won't leave us be!'

'Come now!' a man in bronze shouted back. 'There's no need for panic!'

Túathal crossed to the other side of the courtyard, where a street led away north. He glanced back at the crowd to assure himself that no one had noticed him. A man with braids of dirty blond and grey, standing high on the steps, gestured over the crowd.

'See!' he exclaimed to the weathered old man beside him, who leaned heavily on a staff. 'Listen to your people, Fólki! You should never have agreed to that girl's demands. We should've dealt with her on the spot!'

The old man closed his eyes and frowned, swaying. The clamour of the crowd, the accusations, were clearly too much for him. Túathal took an unconscious step closer, pained that an elder would be treated with such hostility.

But Fólki rallied. Steadying himself, he raised an arm to get the attention of the crowd. The simple gesture quelled the uproar almost at once. His voice was so soft and breathy, Túathal couldn't make out the words from where he stood. He glanced quickly between the street and the crowd. Clicked his tongue and slunk closer, holding the collar of Bo's coat stiff around his face.

'…will rectify our error,' Fólki was saying. 'I hereby revoke Brenna's protection. We will send a troop of watchmen to capture her and bring her back to face the Council's judgement.'

The crowd cheered.

Túathal breathed a sigh of relief and slipped back to the mouth of the street. They weren't going to chase after Fiadh. He didn't understand why, but it seemed the people thought this Brenna was more dangerous than the wolf. That *she* was somehow responsible.

But that had nothing to do with him. He just needed to find Fiadh and calm her like he had before. He'd apologise for what he had done, for what he'd wanted to do. Then, together, they would find their answers.

He ducked down the street, moving swiftly so as not to get caught in the dispersing crowd.

⌘

Túathal found the town's northern gate closed and bolted. Watchmen in the same grey-and-bronze uniforms he'd seen before guarded the heavy doors.

Fiadh mustn't have come this way, then. He followed the wall around to the eastern side of the town, keeping to the shadows, and trailed along it until he was back to the southern district. Back to the ruins. Here, the wall ended in a crumpled mass of debris. What was the point in closing off the front gate, he wondered, with such a gaping breach this side of the town?

He clambered over the rubble, careful of his hands and feet, and down the other side. Out beyond the wall, the land sloped upwards to the high hill on which the lighthouse stood, a black shadow stamped upon the stars.

Túathal dropped his eyes to the snowy ground. He caught his breath. There were prints in the snow – not human footprints. The muddy earth under the ruined wall was kicked up as if something had landed heavily, then bolted away. Moving along, he saw more prints, leading northeast into the night.

Slowly, Túathal straightened, face turning towards the sea. He took a step in its direction. He could hear singing. His people, his brothers, were singing. He took another step. The tide was calling them home. Calling him, as it had called the brides earlier that evening. He felt it, a gentle but insistent pull in his chest.

Home. With Quillen and Dula and the rest. With Ciat, his father.

When the grooms returned to their islands, the celebrations for the newlyweds would last until the full moon. His father would be disappointed that his son hadn't found a bride, but he would smile and hug Túathal and welcome him home. They'd dance, and in a few seasons they would celebrate again. Celebrate the births of the next generation of pups. Túathal wouldn't have his own, but he'd hold Quillen and Dula's and join in the naming of the child.

And he would be wary. Warier than he had ever been before. So that child, that generation, would never lose a parent to the greed of pelt-stealers.

Túathal pulled up short. He'd walked away from the breach in the wall without thinking about it, overwhelmed by the pull of home. He forced his feet to retrace his steps.

He couldn't go. He couldn't abandon Fiadh.

But if he didn't go now, the rest of the grooms would arrive at the islands without him. What would Ciat think? Would he believe he'd lost his son, as well as his wife?

'I'm sorry, Pa,' Túathal breathed, breath misting white in the chill air. 'I'll follow the tide soon, I promise. But if I can't bring Mamma back to you...'

Retracing his steps, he found Fiadh's prints again, sharp eyes picking them out easily even in the dark.

'The least I can do is help Fiadh find her way home.'

30

DARKNESS swallowed the woods beneath a rolling, billowing sea of cloud. Even the snow, so white and dazzling in the day, was dark grey. The trees were almost black. But as Brenna weaved through the sparse edge of the woods, the darkness held no fear for her. Her lantern cast a swaying, flickering circle of amber light before her. It licked up the trunks and bare branches of the trees she passed through. Flung long, pale bars against the knotted forest to her left, down the sweeping slopes of blanketed grasslands to her right.

The tension that had kept her out in the open tremored in her chest. Yet the hand holding her lantern was steady. She thought she could almost hear snatches of a familiar, eerie song. Perhaps it was only the wind as it rushed over the grass, as it curled in the sea-caves. She felt, though she couldn't identify what told her so, that something was gathering. Something was rising, preparing to surge after her, knock her over, drag her into the depths. Was it the storm brewing in the heavy clouds? The weight of their burden dragged them low, so close that Brenna might've been able to reach them, to lose her fingers in their black wool.

A snowflake swirled into the smoke of her lantern. Another, and another. Alighting on her hair, her shoulders, even her lashes. Soon, they would cover the tracks.

What tracks?

Brenna frowned and stopped. *The tracks I've been following.*

I didn't find any.

151

Then why am I out here? Have I… have I been dreaming?

Brenna rubbed her eyes, pinched the bridge of her nose. Looked up and out once more. Lowered her lantern and swept it in a slow arc around her feet, searching for the tracks she must've been following. After all, she wouldn't have forged on in the dead of night for no reason.

Pursing her lips, she crouched. Her bitten leg twinged. She'd been pushing herself all day and now again into the night. Ignoring the ache, she cast about the snow, but it was hopeless. More and more snowflakes swirled in the singing wind. If she didn't find the tracks now, she might lose the trail for good — if there *were* any tracks to begin with. She clicked her tongue and started to straighten up.

A sudden pang raked her thigh. Gasping, she fell back, her leg buckling under her weight. Her lantern swung dangerously, but she just managed to keep hold of it.

Brenna cursed. *Stupid leg.* She gritted her teeth and dragged herself over the snow-covered earth, her naked hand numb and fumbling. Her body ploughed a deep furrow in the snow. She reached for the nearest tree. Put her lantern down to haul herself up, using the tree as a support.

Then she saw it. A grey blur streaked across the grasslands. The glare from her lantern, paradoxically, obscured its details, but Brenna was certain.

She thrust away from the tree, staggered to the next. Now the lantern was behind her and her body masked its light. She peered through the gloom, squinting against the wind. The shape, a pale smudge against the black and grey, slowed from a run to a walk. The fine hairs on the nape of Brenna's neck pricked. She tensed, her fingernails clawed in the tree's damp, coarse bark.

The wolf. So close. Had it sensed her? Had it smelled her?

Remaining still, she focused her attention on the wind. Closed her eyes and pursed her lips. Felt the wind on her face, playing with locks of her hair. Breathed a sigh of relief. She was downwind — the wolf shouldn't be able to pick up her scent.

With a jolt, she realised that wouldn't matter. Not if it saw her light. She fought the impulse to whirl around and scoop up the lantern. A sudden movement might attract its attention too.

She flicked her eyes to look behind her. Slowly, biting her lip, she turned her head to follow. The lantern rested, its base a shadowed island in the pool of its own light, slightly tilted in the troubled snow.

She couldn't reach it without stepping back and kneeling. Her leg would protest, but if she didn't want to face further injury in those red jaws, it would have to be done. Gradually, she sank down the tree, her thigh screaming, her teeth gritted. Eased herself to sit in the snow. Twisted around and reached for the lantern.

Her fingertips brushed the wire handle. It tilted and fell, with a high squeal and glassy *ting*, against the globe.

She winced. Held her breath. Glanced back to the snow-covered plain between the woods and the cliffs.

Her eyes scoured the blackness for that smudge of pale grey, but it was nowhere to be seen.

⌘

Their torches stained the falling snow red. The tramp and crunch of their boots growled like low thunder. Túathal paused on the crest of the lighthouse hill and looked back below. Sjavaba's distant lights flickered from lanterns and filmed windows, like fallen stars dying in the frozen night. The watchmen's torches, however, shone boldly as the troop poured through the northern gate.

Túathal pulled his fur pelt and Bo's coat tight across his chest, but not against the cold wind and snow blustering down in drifts. His chill was of a different kind.

They weren't hunting Fiadh, he reminded himself. Pushing them out of his mind, he quickened his pace, wishing his pursuit were through water. He was much faster in that element. As it was, he had to wade through the shin-high snow. The tracks he was following were

153

steadily blurring, fresh snow erasing them, as the tide would wash away prints on the sand.

No, he wouldn't think of that either. He wouldn't think of the crescent beach, nor the fact that Quillen and the rest would be long gone by now, their presence on the shore soon to be eroded by the beckoning tide.

Fiadh. His thoughts would be for her alone.

⌘

Lantern in hand, Brenna clambered to her feet. She set her teeth and forced her leg to carry her out of the thin line of trees, into the open. Casting the lantern high, she swept it in an arc around her as she hobbled to the place where the wolf had been. Her hair tangled in front of her as she spun, as the wind tossed it at its whim. She ran her hand through her curls, holding them back so she could see. The only sign of the wolf were the tracks it had left behind. Already, the flurries of snow were burying them. If she didn't move quickly, she might lose it. Again.

'And what am I going to do about it?' she demanded, her voice thin, barely a whisper in the storm. 'How am I even supposed to catch up to it with this stupid leg? And if I do…'

The memory of the wolf's writhing weight on top of her, those teeth clamped deep in her flesh, her blood weeping out onto the street…

Brenna shuddered. She had only a knife to – no. Now she remembered. She'd left that behind with the rest of her pack. So she had nothing. Nothing with which to kill it.

She looked down at the tracks. Followed them with her eyes until they faded into the gloom. Shoved aside the doubts crowding in on her and took a step. Bent in on herself as the hastening wind blew about her. Took another step.

She wouldn't worry about it. She would do what she had to, when she had to.

But first, she had to find the wolf.

31

TÚATHAL squinted through the snowfall. Up ahead, he saw a splash of auburn flickering in the dappled grey of the storm. He couldn't tell what it was at a distance, or even whether it was moving or still. He seemed to be gaining on it. As he approached, he realised it was a young woman, her mane of red hair buffeted by the relentless wind.

She couldn't be a watchman, he thought, although he could only see her back. Her clothes were the wrong colour. And the light she held was small and yellow, not the bright red of the watchmen's torches.

As he came closer, his gaze flickering down every now and then to the trail he was following, he saw the figure dip, crouching. The light disappeared behind her.

⌘

Brenna clutched the lantern close to her body. Prising her fingers from the handle, she cupped her palms around the heated glass globe, willing the tongue of flame to lick the stiff cold from her fingers. She bent her head over the globe. The flame danced and fluttered, pulsing like a heartbeat. Like the lighthouse lantern. Burning the same fuel. The globe like a small, simpler version of the glass lens, now shattered in the beacon tower.

I don't want to think of it.

She closed her eyes, just for a second. The flame's warmth played on her chin. A different fire seethed within her. She gritted her teeth.

Her mind and memories kept dancing in circles.

I don't want to think about him!

Brenna lurched to her feet and spun around, almost slipping in the deep blanket of snow. The guttering yellow light, shadowed by her fingers, caressed an approaching figure. It lifted an arm to shield its eyes. She squinted through the dimness, her breaths rasping shallowly, her heart hammering.

A man?

He ducked out of the light and swirled around her. If not for the whisper-rustle of his coat and the dry crunch of his feet through the snow, she might've thought him a wraith, a shade. She whirled to keep him in view, but he remained a shadow in the corner of her eye. She gasped. Felt something tangle and pull through her hair, like some curiously pawing animal. Felt fingers pinch at the hems of her clothes. Heard breaths puff near her ear, as she twisted again to catch the stranger in her gaze.

The light danced and fluttered in her hands. The stranger was close. His salty, murky scent washed over her, as if she'd been dunked into the churning tide. She grunted, her hand shooting out to clamp on the elusive shade. He writhed in her grip, but she bit her nails into his skin and held firm. Her other hand thrust the lantern up into the air so its light cascaded upon the man's head.

Snowflakes crusted his hair. He was bundled in a leather coat over what looked like another garment made of patchy fur. But the arm she held in her grip was bare to the elbow, the leather coat's sleeves blowing empty in the wind. Something about his skin seemed odd, she thought, as her eyes flicked over the stranger. The coloration, the unusual markings… the effect of weak light and heavy shadows, perhaps.

'Enough of – whatever that was!' she spat, fury masking her bewilderment. 'Who are you? What are you doing out here?'

He raised his eyes to meet hers and she almost dropped the lantern. She caught her breath. His *eyes.*

'I'm looking for… a wolf,' he said. And his voice… the husky depths of it. A cadence lower, but just as rich and beautiful and melodious.

Brenna shook herself and focused on his answer, rather than his unnerving appearance.

'*You're* hunting the wolf?' she repeated, the words finally penetrating. Her mouth fell agape. Rallying herself, she straightened her shoulders. 'No.' She shook her head. 'It's my quarry, you hear? I have something to prove to the Council of Sjavaba. So don't you dare get in my way!'

'The Council?' The man frowned. The word apparently held little meaning for him. Abruptly, his expression cleared and he leaned closer. So close Brenna flinched and took a step back. 'Are you Brenna? You're the one they're looking for?'

'What?'

'They're looking for you.'

'Who? The Council? Why?'

The man opened his mouth to answer, but Brenna wasn't listening. Blood roared in her ears. Despite the wind, despite the snow, despite the fact that she was almost numb to her knees, her boots and trousers wet through, a dangerous warmth flushed through her. Hot and fierce as fire.

'They've changed their minds,' she whispered. 'They can't. They *granted* it! I have until full moon!'

The man's eyes stared at her, two becalmed wells. Still and deep. A chill swept over her, like wind over a grass plane. She recoiled, snatching her hand from his wrist. Took a step back. Back from the spectre that loomed in the dark, a distorted memory breathing lies. What *must* have been lies.

But she could believe it was true. Could so easily believe that the people who'd condemned her father, who'd stood silent as she'd faced that lingering, festering hate, again and again, had revoked their protection.

'It doesn't matter!' she snapped. 'They can't complain if I kill the wolf—'

The stranger knocked her off her feet, so quickly she hadn't registered the movement. Her shoulder struck the earth hard. Her leg wrenched. She screamed. Pinpricks of heat blossomed under her shirt, where the wounds torn by the wolf's teeth pitted her shoulder. Her hand still clutched the lantern. She swung it awkwardly up at the man, who'd sunk to his knees beside her. He ducked and caught her wrist.

'What the—'

'You will *not* kill the wolf!' His eyes were no longer calm. A fury that echoed her own warred over his face. She saw his teeth gleam, oddly sharp.

Brenna bared her own teeth and struggled to rise. 'I will do what I bloody well have to! Now let go of me!'

He didn't budge. Instead, he grabbed her other arm to hold her down. The tension that had been taut in the air and darkness all night screeched silently, setting her teeth on edge.

Desperation coloured her anger. 'Let me go!'

⌘

The young woman's shouts hurt. She wielded their weight and heft clumsily, hacking deep. Fiadh's words, from when he'd held her in anger. In silent, icy wrath. If he'd let her go when there was still time…

'I'm sorry,' he cried, remorse diluting his rage. 'But please, you mustn't! You mustn't hurt her!'

'There's no time! The tracks will be covered, and the Council—' She shuddered in his grip.

His eyes widened. The troop of watchmen, with their red torches and thundering feet – they wouldn't be too far behind him. They'd moved at a slower pace, stretched out across the plane to systematically search for their prey. If they had her, they'd take her back to the city and close the gates on her murderous intent. It would buy him time to find Fiadh.

'*Let me go!*' Brenna screeched.

'I can't have you hurting her,' Túathal said, hauling her to her feet. He almost lost his footing as she writhed but wrapped an arm around her waist. She bucked and fought, trying to swing the lantern at his brow.

Then, all at once, she stilled.

A howl pierced the smothered air. Long and low. Thin, but distinct. Threaded through the sighing wind.

Túathal laughed. A small, broken chuckle that burbled on his lips, wet with the tears that sprung to his eyes.

Fiadh. She was close. She was calling him! And the ethereal musicality of her call… it took his breath away.

Brenna butted her head into his stomach. He gave a throaty gasp, hold loosening, and she thrust herself away. Roared, as if with pain, but lurched forward regardless. Towards the howl.

'No!' Túathal shouted. He tore after her. Bo's long coat flapped around his calves, the ice-stiff leather and fleece clinging to his legs, making it hard to move.

He clenched his teeth in frustration. Wrenched the coat from his shoulders and flung it down.

⌘

The light bounced. It made the snow-coated grasslands appear to pitch and rock as Brenna sprinted across it. The ground sloped down, the woods melting further and further away on the left. She was running towards the coastline. She could hear the crash and thunder of the sea, pounding against the cliffs.

She should slow down. Watch her footing. But had caution ever been a rewarding friend?

She remembered now. Or realised. Or imagined. It had been the wolf's howls that had called her to rise, thin in the brewing storm winds. Too faint for conscious recognition. Yet she'd answered the call.

160

The strange man was shouting behind her. She didn't know what he said. Didn't care.

She saw the wolf. A smudge, just a blur against the snow and the glowering blackness of the stormy sky. The yellow fingers of lantern light reached tentatively towards it.

She staggered to a wrenching stop.

The wind had changed.

32

ANY doubts Brenna may have entertained that this was another wolf, whose death wouldn't satiate the Council's so-called justice, vanished when it padded silently into her ring of light.

Although their previous encounter had been rapid, panicked, over in a flicker of tearing red and thrashing weight, she recognised it. Remembered it by its white coat and brazen eyes. By its red jaws, now peeling open to reveal gleaming teeth as it took another step closer. Its coat was even whiter, flecked with snow that glistened in the lantern light.

The fire she'd stoked in her chest for this moment was cringing in its coals, cooling in its own smoke.

Well, you found it, she thought, with a touch of self-mockery. *Now what? How in all those fruitless hours of hunting it did you not think of a plan for what you'd do next?*

She heard the shuffling of the stranger's approach behind her, slow and cautious.

'Step back, Brenna.'

She didn't turn. She wouldn't take her eyes off the beast. Its hackles were raised, its ears flipped back.

'She doesn't want to hurt you. She's a predator right now. She moves on instinct alone, but I can calm her.'

We're not far from the cliffs, Brenna thought, blocking out the man's low voice and ignoring its urgent strain. She opened her eyes wide and tried to take in the lay of the land through her peripheral vision, without allowing her eyes to flicker. From where she stood, she saw several grey mounds rising out of the snow between herself and the edge of the cliffs. Outcrops of boulders and toppled stones.

If I can duck past it and get to those outcrops, I might be able to find smaller rocks I can throw… or, if I can corner it between the outcrops and the cliffs, perhaps I can scare it over the edge…

'Brenna!' the man repeated.

'Shut up,' Brenna hissed.

She knew her hands were trembling. She felt the ache in her injured leg, the blood from her arm's weeping wound dampening the fabric of her shirt. She knew she had no weapon. Yet here she stood. Because here she had to stand. This was her final trial. Her last chance to clutch at freedom.

She had never hated the wolf.

'I don't want to kill it,' she murmured, not really caring whether the stranger heard her or not. She pursed her lips and set her jaw.

When have I ever been able to do what I want?

'But I will.'

I have to.

⌘

Túathal leapt for Brenna and grabbed her by the shoulder, wrenching her back. She shrieked in pain. As he threw her behind him, the wolf pounced.

Its teeth lacerated his left calf. Twisting its head, it jerked his leg out from under him. He cried out. Crashed heavily in the snow. Screeching pain gnawed and tore with each of the wolf's vengeful bites.

Túathal scrabbled in the snow as he tried to haul himself back, away from that blind, wild fury. Screams pierced the snow-dampened stillness of the night. Rang against the rocky outcrops. Echoed in his ears. His own screams. Even in the throes of those violent jaws, his vision lanced with red and foggy black, he didn't fight it.

He bit his lip, tasted blood. Stopped his blind, panic-stricken thrashing. Lurched forward. Flung his arms around the wolf's neck. Ran his fingers through the thick, damp fur. Held fast, even as the wolf bucked. Twisted. Dropped his shredded leg to bite his arms. He squeezed her tighter and sucked in a breath, preparing himself to sing—

A rock struck the wolf's side.

It snarled. Reared. Túathal's grasp broke and the wolf staggered back, turning its flaming eyes to the girl who'd hurled the stone.

⌘

Brenna threw herself to her knees again and plunged her hands into the snow, digging furiously for another stone, another weapon.

The wolf's attack on the stranger was like some hideous pantomime, a mocking reenactment of their first encounter. The sudden lunge. The screams. The blood, almost black in the night, spilling into the churned snow. And the onlooker, watching the scene unfold. She would *not* play that part. Would never play the part of a bystander, standing at a distance and staring. She refused to watch without lifting a hand to help.

Her fingertips grazed something hard.

'No!'

Brenna jerked around. Her hair billowed around her face, in her eyes. She scooped it back. The wolf had released the strange man's leg and turned to her again. Its teeth and muzzle were stained red.

Heart in her throat, Brenna scratched at the frozen earth, trying desperately to dislodge the rock she'd uncovered. The man was screaming, but she couldn't make out the words. Blood roared too loudly in her ears. Was he shouting a warning? Screaming in pain? Calling to the wolf to yield?

Now she could hear it running towards her. The snow muffled the drum of its paws. The space between her hammering heartbeats seemed to slow to hours. Her fingers moved with painful slowness, stiff and numb. The rock wouldn't break free. There was no time. The tension strumming in the air, shivering through her, swelled to a piercing, tooth-edged height.

She gave up on the rock. Snatched up her lantern in both hands. A flicker of movement snagged the corner of her eye as she turned. Without hesitation, she swung her lantern in a big, sweeping arc.

The tension snapped.

The glass globe shattered on the wolf's shoulder. The reservoir of oil cracked. Shards of glass burst asunder in a spray of winking light. A sliver nicked her arm, another glanced her cheekbone. Several more pierced the wolf's flank as it fell heavily to the side. Oil spattered the pelt, streamed down Brenna's arms.

The wolf yelped. Tongues of flame licked up from where the lantern had struck. Raced up its fur, flared where the oil had spilt. Brenna reeled back as the fire leapt high. The wolf whined, howled. Trampled a drunken circle, running from the flames that bit savagely into its side and licked up its neck.

Brenna stared, transfixed. Horrified. The mangled lantern fell from her limp hand.

'FLADH!'

⌘

Túathal's shriek ripped his throat raw. Ignoring the pain, ignoring the blood pulsing down his leg, he scrambled to his feet. The fire leapt and glowed brilliant gold, a beacon that burned all else to utter blackness. He blundered towards the wolf, dragging his useless leg. Smoke billowed from the fire that crawled through the wolf's fur. The new-fallen snow at its feet melted and its desperate writhing trampled the earth and snowmelt to mud. Brenna stood as if petrified, bathed in the light of her reckoning. Her hair glowed amber and sparked gold, a twin flame.

The wolf screamed. A brutally human cry that rent Túathal's heart. He tried to call her name again, but found he was choking, sobbing. He lunged forward but couldn't get close to her side. She was tossing and struggling too wildly and the fire burned too hot. He coughed, eyes streaming. Heard shouting in the distance, back the way they had come. The watchmen had caught up to them.

Too late.

Too late to stop Brenna, to take her away.

Too late to save Fiadh.

Too late to bring his mamma home.

Suddenly, he sprang into the roiling smoke. Brenna cried out. Started forward but failed to grab him before he leapt. He ducked and thrust his hands into the mud. Gathered up an armful and splattered it on the wolf's burning flank. Then he wrapped his arms around her. Lifted her, struggling, into his arms. Pain sluiced agonisingly through his injured leg, but he fought through it.

Brenna shouted. The watchmen yelled. The snowmelt slipped under his feet. The fire flickered and danced, only partially extinguished. His own pelt started to smoke. He didn't stop. Not even when he reached the lip of the cliff.

'Don't!'

He glanced over his shoulder. Brenna had fallen to her knees in the mud. Her hand stretched out towards them, her face contorted with anguish.

Behind her, a line of red torches rushed in, like a mounting wave.

⌘

No pity softened his black eyes. In only a glimpse, she saw them glazed with hatred.

And then he was pitching forward. Falling. He and the wolf together. Over the precipice and into the vengeful sea.

33

TÚATHAL didn't have time to toss his hood over his silver head before they plunged into the ice-cold waters. The shock of the impact knocked the wolf out of his arms. He barrelled deep into the inky blackness, spinning head over heels. He kicked out to check his descent. The waters surged violently around him, preparing to dash him against the cliffs.

He drew his hood deftly over his face. At once, his pelt reacted, swallowing up his skin. His eyes blinked open in a longer, narrower, whiskered face. He kicked his tail. Beat the water with his paddle-like arms. Shot through the blackness, fighting the current. Searching the chaotic waters with heart-clenching fear.

He almost didn't see her. He'd been expecting another shape. But when he spotted the feathery form, glowing pale against the gloom, he recognised her.

Túathal darted down. A string of bubbles and ribbons of something dark twined along his body. His mind was racing twice as fast as his descent. She wouldn't be able to hold on to him. He would have to grab her. But if he shed his seal skin, he wouldn't be able to swim fast enough.

Sorry, Fiadh!

Túathal twirled under her sinking figure and caught her arm in his mouth. He struck out against the waters. Winced, feeling Fiadh's body jerk at the sudden movement. Clamped his jaw, pained that he had to hurt her even more.

167

They broke the surface, churned white as snow. Túathal shook off his hood. Wrapped one arm around her torso, kept them afloat with the other. He'd averted his eyes before, too focused on catching her, too afraid of what he might see. But in the breath between resurfacing and striking out once more, he mustered the courage to properly look at her.

The laugh warbled in his throat. Or it might have been a sob.

She was human. Her eyes were closed. Her head lolled on his shoulder. He couldn't tell if she – no. No time for doubt or dread.

He turned away from the cliffs, swimming as fast as he could with his burden. Ducked under waves that threatened to fling them back and shatter them against the rocks. His powerful strokes pulled them further out to sea. When he felt it safe, sensed it as if the tide whispered so in his ear, he changed direction, swimming parallel to the cliffs. He pulled Fiadh's arms over his shoulders so they clasped around his neck. Flung his hood up. His body rippled and changed.

In his seal skin, he moved much faster. He skimmed close to the surface of the water for Fiadh's sake. Her grip around his neck was weak and he felt a pang of fear, fear that she would slip from his back, would sink into the night-black depths. But all he could do was swim towards the crescent beach.

The tide called. Soft, barely perceptible, but insistent. It sang in his ear and tugged at his body, beckoning him home, swelling until he could no longer ignore it. He gritted his teeth and fought the nigh-irresistible urge to follow its coaxing pull, that ebb and flow he'd lived by for so long.

Fiadh's body slithered backwards and Túathal tore off his hood. His seal form melted into his human skin. He lunged for her hand. Caught it. Hauled her back to his side. Readjusted his grip and held her tight. He couldn't risk changing again, despite this body's limitations in the water.

'Hold on, Fiadh. We're almost there,' he panted, craning his neck. And he spoke true. He saw the curve of the basalt cliffs, the welcome sweep of the glitter-black shore. Heard the curl and crash and fizz of the waves breaking on the sand. Surrendered to the waves, which guided them closer and closer to the crescent beach, until at last it cast them onto the satin sand with a trailing lace of foam.

On his knees, Túathal towed Fiadh up the bank. His breaths came in shallow, shuddering gasps, but she was still. Still and cold as ice. How could someone whose skin had been aflame bare minutes ago be so cold? He traced the frail line of her jaw with his eyes, down her neck and shoulders to her side, where the fire's bite marks blossomed. It had rippled her skin, flaying it to a choppy sea of raw red and pink.

Suddenly, Fiadh's whole body convulsed. She coughed, water spilling out of her blue-lipped mouth. Túathal cried out in relief. But her eyes didn't open. She started to tremble violently.

'Almost there!' he babbled, nearly sobbing. 'You've been so strong. Just be strong for a little longer, *please!*'

Túathal cast his eyes urgently up the beach. It was bare and smooth. Empty of life, of help. He glanced over his shoulder.

The cliffs rose behind him in layered steps. Setting his jaw, he gathered Fiadh into his arms.

⌘

Túathal stumbled up the path to the lighthouse, his shins and elbows slick with blood from his climb. Fiadh shook in his arms, but he clung to her with bitter resolve.

Setting his shoulder to the lighthouse door, he rammed it in. He almost collapsed but forced himself to push on the last few steps, finally sinking onto the threadbare rug in a puff of ash and dust.

He snatched the little pouch that hung from Fiadh's neck. Ripped it open and tipped the treasures out. Seized the flints. Shuffled to the dead grate and clacked them together. Struck them against one another, over and over. But they shed no sparks. Only shrieked as he beat them together. He gave a cry of frustration and grief. Threw them down. Whipped around to face Fiadh.

169

'It's okay – you're going to be all right!' He lunged across the floor and caught up the blanket he'd left discarded by the scullery the afternoon before. It felt a season ago. 'Here!' He scooped her up and wound the cloth around her. 'Fiadh, come on. Please look at me. We're back at the lighthouse. You're safe. And you're in your own skin! The wolf is gone, Fiadh, it's gone! You'd be excited… please…'

He felt the convulsions racking her body ease. Looked down at her, his heart stuttering with hope. But it was misplaced. Fiadh's chest scarcely moved. Her breathing was so shallow he feared she wasn't breathing at all.

Shakily, he raised a hand to her face. Caressed her ashen cheek with tremulous fingers. Her skin was cold to his touch. 'Fiadh,' he crooned, rocking her. Tears warmed the corners of his eyes. Pooled in his lashes. Rolled down his cheeks. 'I… I'm sorry. I should've let you go. My anger… I didn't mean to… I'm so sorry.'

Folding her into his embrace, he pressed his face into the curve of her neck. His shoulders shook even as her shivering body grew still. Even as she slipped away. And all he could offer her was the feeble warmth of his skin.

34

BRENNA looked down at her hands. In the burgeoning dawn light and the glow of the watchmen's torches, the oil staining them looked like blood. *It may as well be*, she thought dully.

Blinking, she fixed her eyes ahead. The watchmen were leading her back to Sjavaba, her wrists bound. Two flanked her, half-holding, half-dragging her. Every step jarred her bitten leg. The rest marched before and behind her in a procession. She might have laughed at the number of men they'd sent after her.

They'd bound her with hesitant hands and wide eyes. Had used loud, gruff voices to veil their uneasiness and distaste. She could've laughed at their fear, too, if she hadn't felt so afraid herself. Afraid *of* herself.

The man had called Fiadh's name. When the fire had flared and the wolf had screamed.

Fiadh. The girl with taut, milky skin and tangled hair. With bare feet and a rich pelt of white fur. The girl with violet eyes and dirt-crusted nails. Who'd reached out her hands to clasp Brenna's, her pinched face soft with a knowing smile, with the understanding Brenna had yearned for.

Why had he called that name?

Maybe I misheard him.

She staggered in the watchmen's grip. They yanked her harshly upright. She barely noticed. Her mind felt detached from her body, in the throes of her thoughts. She'd been in shock at the time. Appalled

171

at what her own hands had wrought. And in that confusion she had thought… only for a moment, but…

She shook herself. It couldn't be.

But why had the stranger cared so much for a wolf? He'd called it "she". Had spoken of it as one does a person. And the hatred in his face had been too raw and strong for the death of a mere beast.

Brenna's heart felt cold when she remembered it, like a chunk of ice weighing down her chest. She recognised that hatred. She'd felt it herself, when her father had stood in the middle of their home, filthy with violence.

She became aware that the watchmen were marching uphill. Her eyes came into focus. The unbroken snow before them blushed pink in the light of the morning sun, their bodies casting long, purplish shadows up the hill.

She turned her head. The lighthouse stood, broken and lonely, on its cliff.

If you need to find me, Brenna, I'll be at the lighthouse.

A keen longing roused within her. Suddenly, it was as if she'd woken from a dream. Everything snapped into vivid focus. The crisp snow under her boots. The coarse ropes around her wrists. The sighing of the wind, the steady thunder of the sea.

She glanced at the watchmen either side of her. Their eyes were shadowed, their movements stiff and unrefined. She looked up again at the lighthouse, gleaming in the fresh sunlight. She needed to get there. Needed to see her friend, to assure herself that she hadn't done what she feared.

She twisted her hands helplessly against the knotted bonds. But how? With watchmen before her and behind? Once they took her through the northern gate to the Council…

Well. She entertained no hope that they'd allow her to ride back out with the promised horse and cart.

Brenna closed her eyes and let her legs buckle. The watchmen on either side of her grunted as her sudden collapse lurched them off balance. They tried to pull her upright, but she refused to carry her own weight. With her eyes shut and her head hung low, it must've looked as though she'd fainted.

'What's going on?' a voice called from the back of the line.

'She's collapsed!' the watchman to her right shouted back.

'What's the hold up?' asked someone ahead.

'She. Has. *Collapsed!*' the man bit out agitatedly. 'What should we do?'

'Carry her!'

'You're joking.'

'Don't speak back!'

The man muttered something under his breath. He and the watchman on Brenna's left side bent to lift her body. She heard the men who'd formed the tail end of the procession overtake them, as her captors hefted her up roughly. The movement agitated her injured leg and shoulder and she almost grunted.

They resumed their march. As they strode up the slope of the lighthouse hill, she focused on the upward motion. She'd have to be alert to get the timing right.

She felt the change when they reached the crest of the hill. Holding her breath, she attuned herself to the rhythm of their footsteps, so she'd know when they started going down the other side.

Their footsteps faltered slightly. Snow hissed downhill. She counted. One… two… *three!*

Brenna snapped her eyes open and punched up with her bound fists. Her knuckles cracked into the unsuspecting watchman's chin and his head flew back. At the same time, she curled her legs in and struck out, kicking into the second watchman's chest. The sudden attack loosened their hold on her and she squirmed free.

She fell heavily. Groaning, she rolled onto her stomach and pushed herself up. The man she'd punched had already fallen and lay unmoving in the snow. With a great effort, she shoved the second man so he lost his footing and fell, slipping and sliding, down the slope.

She heard cries below as he barrelled into the rest of the troop. She hoped he knocked over at least a few of them but didn't waste time making sure.

Staggering back up to the crest of the hill, she retraced the watchmen's boot prints. Twisted her oil-slicked wrists, bit at the knots, and managed to slip her hands free.

Now she realised how little she'd thought her plan through. When the watchmen disentangled themselves and gave chase, any prints she left in the new snow would lead them straight to her.

She glanced with frustration at the lighthouse. The prison she'd sworn never to return to. The looming reminder of all she'd possessed, all she'd lost, always casting its shadow over her. Yet now she'd decided she must go back to it, it seemed impossibly far away. She ignored the impulse to just sprint to it across the blank snow and instead ran over the path of prints the watchmen had made, back down the eastern side of the hill.

She heard the disordered tramp of the watchmen's boots and knew she'd have to think quickly. On her right, the snow-capped grasslands fell away into the sea. She veered off the beaten path, over to the cliff, skidding to a sharp stop. Peering over the lip, she saw the basalt pillars drop away in layered, hexagonal steps to a sweeping shore of black sand. The uneven ledges curved all the way around to the cliff atop which the lighthouse was built.

With only a moment to conceive the next step of her plan, Brenna stripped off her coat and flung it over the edge. Scrambled down onto the basalt steps. Turned around, braced her hands and lowered herself down, until her head was about two feet below the lip. Started edging along the cliff, towards the lighthouse. Her fingers felt swollen with cold, slick with lamp oil. They scrabbled clumsily on the stone and she had to dig them firmly into the cracks to hold herself in place. Her hair whipped about her, making it hard to see, and her numb feet almost slipped several times on the frost-slick steps.

A strong wind blew off the ocean, buffeting her against the rocks.

She froze, clinging in place. Her teeth chattered. She pressed on, ears straining for the sound of the watchmen cresting the hill or clattering down the slope, but with the wind blustering in her ears, she couldn't hear a thing.

She pictured them scouring the white-blanketed grasslands for her prints and seeing the point where she'd ploughed off the path. If they followed the tracks to the cliff and looked over the edge, she hoped that her reddish-brown coat would stand out against the black sand and catch their eyes, so they wouldn't turn and see her, picking her faltering way along the wall like a wounded mountain goat. It wouldn't buy her long, but she hoped it'd be enough of a distraction for her to steal back up the cliff and into the lighthouse unseen.

Brenna risked a backwards glance. She had to prise one hand from the rocks to drag her wind-tossed hair out of her eyes. It felt like she'd been crawling along the wall for an age, so she was surprised when she saw not even a shadow peeping over the lip where she'd slipped down.

The orange dawn peered through ribbons of dark grey cloud. The sun was high enough now that its light caressed the top of the cliffs, its peach glow creeping down towards her. If it caught in her hair and set her red curls alight, they'd be as bold a beacon as any the lighthouse had cast.

But she'd have to chance it. And soon, she realised – the lighthouse tower was right above her!

She inched up the cliff, heart fluttering painfully in her throat. If any watchmen were looking her way – or if they were behind her, searching the sands below – surely they'd see her scurry over the edge and dart to the lighthouse.

If they do, they do, she told herself doggedly. Steadied her breathing. Flexed her fingers and toes.

Someone gave a shout.

Brenna leapt into action, as if the cry had been a signal. She scaled the basalt steps as fast as her beaten body allowed. Hauled herself over the lip and rolled onto her feet. Then she was running. She moved with a crooked gait but didn't slow.

Inspiration struck her and she veered around the back of the lighthouse. The snow cover was scanter here. When the tower's shadow fell over her, she bent and wrenched off her boot. Jammed it, toe-first, in the muddy earth at the edge of the cliff, as if she'd tripped and hurtled over the precipice. Skirted the base of the tower, trying not to step in the snowdrifts or muddy patches. Trying not to leave a trace.

Suddenly, she was on the doorstep, her palm on the handle, the handle twisting, the door swinging inwards. All at once, as though time was spilling through her fingers like fast-moving water. She wanted to slow the torrent, stop the flow. This was a haunted place. A place that had witnessed harrowing things, its memories seeping from the cracks in the walls, whispering in the timbers of the rafters. To step inside it again…

But her body moved faster than her burdened, sluggish mind. She'd already flown over the threshold. The door cracked loudly on the wall and ricocheted, its hinges squealing. It slammed shut behind her.

Brenna didn't know exactly what she'd expected to see. Perhaps Fiadh sitting on the woven rug next to the fireplace, or pottering about in the scullery, blithely unaware of the night's events. Perhaps she half-expected an empty room strung with crystallised cobwebs, proof that the girl she'd seen in the woods had been a spectre all along.

Whatever she might've anticipated, it was not the scene she burst in on. The strange man she'd met in the dark and snow, huddled on a threadbare rug in front of the dead fireplace. Water ran down his arms and legs, dripped off his hair and fur garment. He crushed a pale figure to his body. Her sodden cream-coloured hair fell in tangles around her ashen face. She was bundled in a darkly stained blanket. The man bled from grazes on his forearms and deep lacerations on his calf. The rug drank the blood, as if it were watered wine.

The man raised his head. He was shaking with hacking sobs. Tears rolled down his patchy cheeks. His eyes were impossibly round, impossibly black. He stared through her.

'I couldn't save her,' he rasped.

35

BRENNA stared, almost unable to comprehend what she was seeing.

'Fiadh?' she whispered. Falteringly, on uneven feet, she crossed the room and sank to her knees beside them. Reached out her hands to Fiadh, to brush the hair back from her deathly pale face.

The man snatched Fiadh even more tightly into his embrace. He bared his teeth at Brenna, suddenly alert. 'Don't touch her!'

She ignored him. Her mind was still struggling to keep up with what was happening. She unwound a fold of the damp blanket. Shuddered, eyes fixed on the terrible, blistering wound that licked up Fiadh's shoulder and neck. Describing the fire Brenna had smashed across the wolf's skin.

Tears stung Brenna's eyes. Hand trembling, she brushed her forefinger down the hollow curve of the girl's cheek. 'She's so cold. How can she be so cold?'

'She's dying!' The man flung the words at her with blunt abandon. 'Because of you! Because—' Ferocity melting, he hid his face in Fiadh's still chest. He sobbed. 'Because of me.'

Brenna blinked. 'No,' she breathed. Then, louder, 'No!' She shook her head stubbornly and sprang up. 'Not if I have anything to say about it!'

It's smaller than I remember — the bed we shared is covered in dust — I forgot the tiles are uneven.

She brushed away the thoughts that manifested about her old home like pale, whispering ghosts. Found the clothes chest at the foot of the bed, where she'd known it would be. It was overturned and the latch was broken. She flung the lid open and scooped out old, moth-eaten clothes. Her fingers scratched the sides, searching for the rope handles, feeling her father's carvings. Seals and ships and merrily curling waves. It had been his wedding gift to her mother. His carvings had always been charming. A paradox. A testament to the beauty wicked hands could create.

Finding the handles, she hauled the chest across the room, its edge squealing against the slate. The strange man watched her, dumbfounded, as she dropped the chest and circled to the fireplace. She took up the poker, raised it high, and swung it down with all her strength.

The chest cracked like an eggshell. She smote it again. It groaned and splintered, boats breaking apart, seals and surf churning together until one couldn't be told from the other. Brenna flung the pieces into the cold grate. Her hand swept over the top of the mantelpiece but came away coated with dust. Cursing, she bolted to the scullery and rooted through the drawers. A family of mice scurried out, fleeing from her clamouring search. Finally, she caught up a tiny, crumpled box with nibbled corners. Flew back to the fireplace, fell jarringly to her knees, and struck a match. Within moments, a fire flared in the grate.

'Bring her closer! We have to get her dry and warm.'

The man stared at her. In the golden light flickering from the newborn flame and the honeyed glow of the scullery window, she could see him clearly for the first time. The odd coloration she'd noted vaguely in the dark… he was mottled silver with patches of fawn and black.

'You're helping her?' he asked slowly. Conflicting emotions warred on his silver-and-fawn face.

'Yes. Now hurry!'

Spurred into obedience by the sharpness of her voice, the man shuffled forward, steam rising off his body. They both looked down at Fiadh's face. No expression creased her glistening brow. She looked like a corpse.

Brenna ran her hands through her mane. 'This won't be enough. She—' Her eyes flicked to the man at her side, bloody and bruised. 'You *both* need a healer.'

'Bo,' he murmured.

'What?'

'Someone down among the human dwellings.'

'I know who Bo is. *You* know him?'

His hand shot out and gripped her arm. His eyes were wide with hope. 'Go get him. Please!'

'I – I can't. He hates me. They *all* hate me.'

He hesitated only a second. 'Tell him it's me asking. Tell him Túathal… wait, I don't know if he'll remember my name. He called me Silver. Tell him—'

Brenna was already nodding. She burned to ask how this stranger knew Bo, but there was no time to waste on niceties. She stood up but stopped abruptly, looking down at herself. No coat. One boot. Masses of red curls. She wouldn't get anywhere near the apothecary's store if the watchmen caught her.

'Why are you—'

'Wait.'

She went to the back of the room and rooted through the assortment of clothing on the floor. Stripped off her clothes, which were streaked with blood, dirt, and oil stains. Quick as her weary limbs allowed, she donned one of her mother's old winter slips and a pair of thick woollen stockings. Slipped into an oversized shirt and belted it at the waist. Swung a dusky cloak around her shoulders and pulled on a pair of scuffed boots. Last, she bound her hair with a ragged scarf and tugged a cap on over the top.

Dressed again, she limped over to the rug. Perhaps it was the flickering firelight, but she imagined some colour had returned to Fiadh's cheeks.

She reached for the other girl's hand. Her skin felt paper-thin. Squeezing the bony fingers, Brenna pressed them to her lips, oblivious to Túathal's wary gaze.

'Fiadh, I beg you,' she whispered fervently. 'Live!'

36

FIADH'S memories of Elowyn were warm, coloured with bright, tender strokes. The yellow of her hair falling loose about her rosy cheeks. The honey-amber of her crinkled eyes. The bruised pink of her work-worn hands, firm and loving as they held Fiadh's, as they wove her hair.

So Fiadh couldn't understand why everything was so cold.

'Ma?' she tried to say, though she couldn't hear her own voice. Her mother's arms folded tight around her, yet still she was swept from those arms, as a boat torn from a safe harbour.

Why was it so cold?

She reached for her mother's skirts, but they swirled like clouds, like ribbons of smoke. Smoke from the fire licking over Fiadh's shoulder. She screamed, but there was no sound. No heat.

Why was it so *cold?*

Her father's rough, scarred hands draped a white pelt around her shoulders. 'It will protect you in my stead,' he told her. But instead of stifling the flames, the pelt caught fire. 'I'm sorry.'

But those words echoed with another, viscous voice. And still she thought she should burn, but still the cold seeped deeper into her flesh. The warm tones whispered into a red-black mist.

Why was it so…

182

A small breath of warmth blushed over her body. Not that of the fire she'd feared. A delicate touch, a tender embrace.

Fiadh let out a shuddering sigh and sank into it.

37

THE watchmen returned to Sjavaba empty-handed. Bo arched an eyebrow when two of them were carried into his grandfather's store and laid out on the cots. One had a red-purple welt on his jaw and dazed eyes. The other had nasty grazes on his hands and a broken leg. He recognised the second as Kasim, the watchman who'd sighted the white wolf the morning after it'd attacked Brenna.

'Well, I'm comforted to know Sjavaba is in such capable hands,' Bo said dryly. 'I clearly underestimated what Brenna was capable of.'

He bent over Kasim to inspect his injuries. With a weary sigh, Yuel came around the screen and started examining the dazed man on the other cot, muttering to himself in his low, breathy voice. Bo peeled back Kasim's shredded sleeves and grimaced at the raw grazes.

'Though, I doubt she was responsible for this.' His eyes trailed to Kasim's crooked leg and he arched his eyebrow again. 'Did you fall?'

Kasim's face was contorted with pain, gleaming with sweat. He grunted yes.

'Bo, how badly hurt is your man?' Yuel asked.

'Broken leg, surface-level grazes on his arms. I'll get the splints.'

'You'll need help to set the bone. Would you all stop *gawping* and blocking the way?'

Straightening, Yuel ushered the lingering watchmen out from behind the screen. He came over to Kasim's bed and Bo slipped past him. As he sidled around the edge of the screens, he tapped the nearest watchman, a slim blond man, on the shoulder.

184

'What happened?' he whispered.

The blond man turned bloodshot eyes to Bo. 'We found the keeper's daughter. There was a tussle of some kind before we caught her. Blood in the snow, and we saw something on fire fall off the cliff.'

'S'that so… the wolf?'

He shrugged. 'Didn't see what it was.'

Bo's hands clenched into fists.

Brenna didn't want this, he thought suddenly. He remembered opening the door to find her nearly crippled on the step. Remembered how she'd pushed past him, unwittingly entering a lair of enemies. And when the crowd had turned on her, raised their voices and fists against her, she'd cowered, scrambled back in vain, pleaded her innocence.

And abruptly, he pictured a much smaller girl. Stocky and freckled. Dragging him to explore the docks. Bouncing at his side as they watched the ships coming and going, an expression of earnest determination on her face. And later… he recalled the girl, a few summers short of womanhood, staring at him in horror as men swarmed her home, armed with violence.

Brenna had only ever wished harm to one man, and even then, she'd never raised her hand against him.

Neither had Bo. But he'd let it happen.

No, Brenna hadn't wanted any of this.

'Where's she being held?' Bo asked casually. 'I want to speak to her.'

The blond man rubbed the back of his neck, looking sheepish. Bo frowned.

'You caught her, right?'

The man grimaced. 'Yes. And we were almost back. Then she clocked Coen on the jaw, shoved Olson, and got away.'

Bo pressed a finger to his chin, trying to interpret the report. 'So… you caught her, you had her, she bested you and ran away, and you couldn't catch her again?'

The man shrugged with an air of defeat. 'She just vanished. We thought she went over the cliffs. Kasim tried to follow, but something startled him and he slipped. By the time we managed to bring him up again, we'd lost her completely.'

Bo opened his mouth to press for more details, but before he could ask the question burning on the tip of his tongue, his grandfather put his head around the screen. 'Bo, would you hurry up with those splints?'

'Of course, *Afi*.'

The blond man hesitated, but Bo jerked his chin at him, giving him permission to leave. He nodded gratefully and followed his fellow watchmen onto the street.

Bo turned on his heel and weaved through the shelves to the back of the shop. Pursing his lips, he drummed his fingers on his thigh.

He hadn't asked the questions he really wanted answered. Had Túathal been there? That "son of the tide", as his grandfather called him.

Had he seen what Brenna had done?

⌘

Brenna didn't risk coming in through the northern gate. Instead, she limped around the wall until she reached the place where it crumbled into rubble.

Scrabbling over the debris, she dropped painfully onto the other side. The sun had barely been up an hour, but already she could hear the distant sounds of the town waking up. She glanced around to get her bearings and set off in the direction of the town square, tugging her cap down a little more firmly over her distinctive hair.

She reached the apothecary's street but turned into the back laneway. The store's narrow facade was pressed between two neighbouring buildings, with no gap between their adjoined walls to slip through. She recognised Yuel's back door, which was painted the same matte black as the front.

Brenna hesitated, nibbling her lip. But then she set her jaw and grasped the handle.

It twisted under her fingers. Gasping, she snatched her hand back. The door swung in. Bo came into view, framed in the doorway. He blinked, eyes flicking up and down, taking in Brenna's mismatched clothes and overall dishevelment.

'Speak of the de—'

Cutting himself off with a curse, he shot a look over his shoulder, pushed her out into the dimness of the laneway, and snapped the door shut behind him. 'What the *hell*, Brenna?'

'Bo,' Brenna panted. 'You've got to help her—'

'Why are you here?'

'Please, there's no—'

'What are you *thinking*? There are watchmen in there. You managed to—'

'—time for you to rag on me. This girl, the wolf, Fiadh, she's hurt—'

'—get away from a dozen of them, just to come—'

'— and she's dying—'

'—waltzing back? Why *did* you come back? Why do you keep coming back here when you *know*—'

'Because you're the only one!' Brenna cried. He flinched. 'You were the only friend I ever had. And I need you, I—'

She faltered. Looked up into his face, the painstaking carelessness lost in knitted brows, stiff mouth. 'I needed you, Bo. I needed you and you just stood there and let it happen.'

Her chest tightened, her throat clenching with the pain of it, the ugly wound as raw as the day it was inflicted. But this wasn't the time. That wasn't the wound. The injuries that needed mending were those she had wrought.

Brenna grasped his arm. 'But that's not why I'm here now. Please, I'm begging you, *help her*. I'm not asking you to be my friend again. You don't have to be my friend. You don't have to like me, even. You can hate me for all I care! I – I don't care, I *don't*. Hate me all you want! But don't hate me because of my father, because of what he did. Because I'm his daughter. Hate me, for *me*, and my own mistakes! Hate me for what *I've* done. Oh!'

She coughed, hot tears smarting her cheeks, spilling into her mouth. She buried her face in her hands. 'Bo. What *have* I done?'

For a moment, there was no answer.

'What you were driven to do.' Bo's voice was surprisingly soft. 'Because *Afi* waited too long to intervene. Because when he did speak, he spoke in grief to others desperate for someone to blame for their pain. Because the Council acted in anger and violence, and no one showed you a hint of compassion. Not even…'

Brenna caught her breath. Raised her face from her hands.

Bo dragged his eyes to hers.

'What I drove you to do,' he finished. And there was no mockery in his angular face, on his usually sharp tongue. He took her hands and drew them from her face. 'That's done. It's happened. But I'm ready now, Brenna.'

Brenna gaped at him. 'You mean…'

He nodded. 'Take me to her.'

38

TÚATHAL reached for Fiadh's hand and twined his fingers with hers, black-brown and milk-white. He heard Bo's words, but they sounded quiet and far away.

'I've done all I can for her,' the apothecary's grandson murmured, rising to his feet. He and Brenna had dragged the mattress from the bed and laid it out before the hearth. Túathal had lifted Fiadh onto it and from there Bo had done his work.

'I'll keep doing all I can, until there's nothing more I can do. Túathal.' The selkie raised his head. 'You've got to let me see to you now.'

Bo's words were gentle, but firm. Túathal nodded and let Fiadh's fingers slip through his. Bringing his bag over, Bo sat next to him on the threadbare rug.

'Brenna, I'll need more water.'

By the time Bo had finished binding Túathal's leg and the grazes on his arms, and finally convinced Brenna to let him see to her reopened wounds, the sun had reached its apex.

'Now, both of you,' Bo said, with a tone that allowed no argument. 'Get some rest. I need to go and let *Afi* know he doesn't have to send a score of watchmen out looking for me, but I'll be back with food and firewood. And when I get back,' he added, raising his eyebrows at them, 'you two better be asleep.'

He pulled the door closed, its click sharp in the silence. Túathal dragged himself across the slate floor until he sat beside Fiadh's mattress. Bo had neatly bandaged her side, shoulder, and neck. Bloodstains already shadowed the white linen, but as Bo had said, it was all he could do.

Once again, Túathal took one of her hands and clasped it in his own.

⌘

Brenna didn't want to stay in the lighthouse. Memories clung to its walls like the cobwebs strung in its rafters. She could imagine she heard her mother's husky voice in the wind as it rattled in the chimney, heard the pad of her bare feet in the creaking and settling of the building's timbers. Could imagine she saw her father's shadow flung against the walls by the tongues of flame in the grate. The flickering fire evoked his erratic movements, his fleet-footed anger.

But she had lit that fire.

Her eyes wandered to Fiadh. She forced herself to look at the bandages that wound up Fiadh's neck and down her arm.

Túathal was curled up beside her. Brenna had felt so drawn to her, had felt so known and understood by her, that it rankled to see him that close, to see his fingers interlocked with hers, while Brenna sat apart. He hadn't looked at Brenna since she'd gone to find Bo. Hadn't spoken a word to her. He too, no doubt, wished she wasn't here.

Not that she could leave either. As Bo had said, the watchmen were still looking for her. The Council needed its scapegoat. Again. At last, Sjavaba had fully rejected her.

She couldn't go back. She couldn't stay here. And she couldn't run away. There was nowhere to run.

The collar of her mother's shift felt suddenly tight around her throat. She raised her hand and tried to ease the constricting fabric, feeling her pulse in her neck, ticking too fast. The cloak was too heavy on her shoulders. Clicking her tongue, she struggled with the clasp until her trembling fingers managed to unhook it. She drew the cloak off and bundled it in her arms.

Brenna looked down at the dusky cloth. It shifted from purple to grey in the contrasting light of the fire and the sun, which filtered in through the scullery window. The fabric was soft in her arms. She rose to her feet, boots scuffing the slate as she moved over to the mattress where Fiadh lay. Túathal raised his head, watched her unblinking as she knelt and spread the cloak over the girl she had burned.

'Thank you.'

Brenna started. She looked at Túathal, but his gaze had wandered to the fire. A lump rose in her throat. 'Don't thank me.'

'Fire confuses me.' His silver skin shone rose-gold in the light of the hearth. 'It's too bright for my eyes. It's too hot. And it destroys. Yet… Fiadh needed it too. It almost killed her, but she needed it to live. I don't understand it.' And now he did look at her and she felt like she could fall into those eyes and drown. 'You almost killed her, yet you also saved her. And I saved her, but almost killed her.'

'Then it would've been better for her if she had never met either of us.'

'No. I don't think that's true.'

Brenna flung up her hands. 'Look at her!' Tears burned in the corners of her eyes. She swiped at them impatiently. 'You said so yourself. She almost died! I almost killed her!'

Túathal shook his head patiently. 'Yes. But instead you freed her.' He squeezed Fiadh's hand. 'The pelt is gone, burned up. The wolf will never wake in her again. You helped her where I could not.'

Brenna stared at him. 'That fur she wore changed her?'

Túathal nodded. 'It made her like me. Able to shift between two bodies. But unlike me, she wasn't born with two skins. She was losing herself to the wolf.'

'And you? What are you?'

Túathal tweaked the edge of his garment's hood. 'A selkie.'

Brenna caught her breath. 'My mother used to tell me tales of selkies… she knew so many songs about them.'

A soft smile touched Túathal's mouth and he leaned closer. 'Of course she did. She was a selkie too.'

Brenna snorted. 'No. What? No. How would you know? You don't know her. You haven't met her.'

The selkie cocked his head. 'I believe I have. Brenna, the lighthouse keeper was your father, wasn't he?'

His words struck her like a physical blow to the stomach. She jumped to her feet, but he kept speaking.

'I didn't realise at first. I didn't even think that they… that they might've had a child. And I didn't recognise you. But then, with the fire, I saw it. How you resembled him.'

Brenna's legs felt like water. She pressed her lips together, trying to summon her fire. The fire that made her bold, that loosened her tongue to snap back. That let her tilt her chin up and fight.

'But I see it now,' he continued in a strangely flat manner. 'You've got his hair.'

'Stop.'

'So if your father was the keeper of this lighthouse, then your mother was Idunn.'

'How do you even…'

'You don't know what he did to her, do you?'

Brenna stiffened. Her mouth hardened to a grim line.

'Don't speak as if you're telling me something I don't know,' she said in a low, dangerous voice. 'I know. Better than anyone. Better than the Council, than Yuel. Than *you*. I know what sort of man my father was.'

There was her fire.

'What happened to her?'

Brenna thrust up her chin. 'She fled. She ran away from him.' Was it insane to feel so proud with those words stinging her lips? Was it right to let the truth that'd caused her so much bitterness raise her head high? 'She escaped.'

Túathal shook his head. 'No. She did not.'

Brenna took a step closer. 'What happened, then?' she snapped. 'If you know so *much* about my family?'

Túathal met her eyes. 'Like I said, she was a selkie, a daughter of the tide.'

'She was a foreigner. From across the sea.'

His black eyes were unwavering. 'Your father stole her pelt so she couldn't return to her home. To her family.'

'He locked her up in the lighthouse.'

'She found her pelt and escaped.'

'Yes! She escaped—'

'He killed her.' His voice was brutally calm.

The floor seemed to pitch beneath her. She shook her head vehemently. 'That's not true. That can't be true. Why are you lying?'

'He ripped her pelt from her—'

'No.'

'—he burned it—'

'No!'

'—and she drowned.'

'*No!*' Brenna screamed. 'You're lying! She got away! She *must* have!'

Tears swamped the selkie's deep eyes as he looked up at her. 'No, she didn't. Your father stole her freedom, broke her spirit, and killed her. I know. I saw. Fiadh saw. I know she didn't make it. If she had, I would've seen my mother again.'

Brenna froze. She looked at him and saw him. His silver-and-fawn skin. His round black eyes. The tears spilling over his cheeks.

She shook her head. As if that might deny the truth she could so clearly see.

She staggered backwards, away from him. She turned. Fled.

But there was nowhere to run.

39

WHEN they'd killed her father, she'd found herself here.

Brenna clung to the railing, the only thing separating her from empty air. Icy wind whipped over the balcony, whistling through the lantern room. Below her, the ocean pounded high up the cliff face, churning the surface of the water to white froth.

Her father had fallen here. The ocean had swallowed him up, then spat his battered body out onto the beach. If what Túathal said was true, she'd lost two parents to this wrathful beast.

She turned her face to the west and looked down at the town. From here, she could see ribbons of chimney smoke and movement as people went on living. She could see the greys and browns of the northern district and the charcoal smudge of the ruined portside. The remnants of a flooding storm.

No… if Túathal was right, she'd lost both parents to fire and men. And all the tide had taken was its vengeance.

'Brenna.'

Her hands twitched on the railing. She turned slowly around. Her curls flowed around her head, ribbons of wind-stirred flame. Her mother's shift billowed around her ankles.

Túathal stood beside the lantern's dais. Idunn's son. She could see it so clearly in the light of day. Her eyes traced the familiar features.

She must have missed him, Brenna thought. It must have pained her not to be able to watch her son grow, year after year trapped in the lighthouse. Brenna's chest ached vaguely.

Her mother's son crossed the glass-scattered floor and stopped on the other side of the lattice windows. An odd expression disturbed his features.

'Why are you here?' she asked flatly. She gestured at the drop behind her. 'Have you come to throw me off? They did that to my father, you know. They said it would "appease the tide", or some nonsense.'

'I'm sorry.' He ran a hand over the latticework until he found the catch and opened the door to the balcony. Stepped through, pelt rippling in the wind. 'I shouldn't have told you in that way. It was cruel.' He took a deep breath. 'You are not the only one to resemble your father.'

Brenna eyed him carefully. 'What do you mean?'

'If the keeper had released my mother, then things would've been different. Last night, when Fiadh was changing, I… I held her back. I knew she was about to change and lose herself. I see the keeper in myself and it sickens me. If I'd let her go, she might have locked herself in here before she changed skins. Then this wouldn't have happened.'

Brenna blinked.

'Changed skins,' she repeated, the words caressing her lips. They tasted light. Heart stirring, she closed her eyes.

Imagine the freedom. To be able to slip into another form, step into another life.

Behind her closed lids, the wolf's wicked jaws burst wide. Her eyes flew open. The taste soured on her tongue.

'Why did you hold her back, Túathal?'

'I was angry.' He looked away from her. 'When I learned that a human had stolen my mother from me, I felt such grief. Such anger. Fiadh said her other skin was dangerous and I…' He twisted his lip in a bitter sneer that looked wrong on his face. 'I wanted to use that danger.'

'You wanted the people to suffer your pain.'

He bowed his head. 'I didn't want that. Not really. Rather…' He stopped himself and pressed his mouth shut, but Brenna knew what he'd almost said.

'You wanted my father to suffer.'

There was a long pause. Túathal twisted his hands. 'In that moment,' he murmured at last, meeting her gaze once more, 'I let my anger hurt Fiadh. I was no better than him. But you didn't mean to hurt her, Brenna. You didn't know she was beneath the wolf's skin. You even tried to protect me.'

Brenna closed her eyes, battling the emotion that made her throat tight. She let go of the rail and crossed the balcony, joining him by the latticework.

They regarded one another in silence. She felt his eyes on her, wandering over her features, taking her in. She knew who he was looking for and smiled sadly to herself.

You won't find our mother in me.

'This is a mess,' she said. Cupping her face in her hands, she found her cheeks wet. She snorted and tried to wipe them dry. But she couldn't. Her eyes pooled with tears, blurring her vision, spilling down her cheeks. Her lips trembled and she pressed the back of her hand against them, holding back the sobs.

'Our mother.' She let the words form on her tongue. Sweet, but with a sharp, bitter edge.

'Our mother,' Túathal repeated. She peered up at him. His liquid eyes wept like hers, but he made no move to wipe the tears away.

Brenna's heart lurched. 'I'm sorry. I'm sorry she never came back to you, Túathal.'

Túathal surged around her, like waters breaking their banks. Pulled her into his arms. Pressed her into his rich pelt, soft and warm. She tensed, eyes wide. 'I'm sorry, Brenna,' he breathed. 'I'm sorry she left you alone.'

A gasping sob escaped her throat. All at once, she found herself hugging his torso, sinking into the comfort of his embrace. Letting her remorse and pain and grief and loss pour out of her, and receiving his in kind.

⌘

Túathal couldn't have said how long they stood on the balcony, harboured in each other's arms.

Eventually, the tears dried on his wind-touched cheeks. His head ached dully from crying. His neck felt stiff. But as Brenna raised her head and turned her swollen, honey eyes up to him, he found his heart strangely calm. Not light. Not unburdened. Just calm. The calm of knowing there was no more to fear, to face. There was only the waiting.

Brenna searched his eyes. He forced a smile, as much to encourage himself as for her.

'Let's go to Fiadh. We have much to apologise for. The least we can do is be together with her when she wakes.'

'And if she…'

Brenna pursed her lips and shook her head, unable to say it.

'If the worst should come to pass' – although his voice quavered, he clung resolutely to that inexplicable peace – 'we will face it together. My sister.'

40

FIADH was walking in a wood. Although it was dark and she held no light, she wasn't afraid, her footsteps light and effortless.

She looked up. The shadow sky was empty. That wasn't right. Something ought to be there.

'*Pabbi?*' she spoke into the blackness.

From the darkness, her father's voice whispered. 'Stars, wild one.'

'Was there ever such a thing?'

'Oh, child. Have you forgotten the stars?'

'I will remember if you show me, *Pabbi*. Where are they?' She lowered her eyes and looked about her. The woods dissolved like smoke, billowed, reformed into shapes, collapsed again. '*Pabbi?*' she called as the blackness swirled about her, tossed by a phantom wind. 'Where are you?'

Suddenly, she was afraid.

She stumbled through the shapeless plane, calling for him. Crying. The shadows scraped her skin, shredded her flesh. With each step, with each tear, she screamed in pain. Hot, crackling pain. Her tongue swelled in her mouth until she could shout no more. She flailed at the preying shadows, one-armed, for the other was unravelling. And the heat stabbed behind her eyes, bled through her skin. It was too much for her to bear.

The wolf!

She sobbed in relief. *Of course!* It was stronger. It was bolder. Fiadh bared her teeth and summoned that lupine companion.

Nothing.

She wrenched her jaw open and screamed.

⌘

'Do something, Bo!' Brenna cried. In her lap, Fiadh's head tossed, and a long, terrible moan escaped her twisted lips. Brenna bent over her and stroked her sweat-dampened hair. 'Shh, Fiadh. Shh, shh. *Please*, Bo!'

'What's the matter with her?' Helplessly, Túathal ran his hands through his curls. 'Why is she screaming?'

'Oh, I don't know. Nothing to do with the burn covering half her back, I'm sure,' Bo bit out tersely.

'You don't have anything to give her for the pain?' Brenna demanded.

'What do you *think* I'm doing?'

Túathal craned forward. Bo was taking one thing after another from his satchel, rolling them in his fingers or sniffing them hastily, before setting them aside. A jar of powder. A drawstring pouch. A clutch of pungent leaves, tied together with twine.

Bo clicked his tongue. Brenna tugged his arm. 'She's waking!'

Bo dropped the satchel. 'Fiadh?' he asked, in a much milder tone. 'Fiadh, can you hear me?'

Fiadh's eyes swivelled under her eyelids. Suddenly, they snapped open. She cast around confusedly until she found Bo's angular face. Parted her chapped lips, but only a dry rasp hissed between her teeth.

Without turning his head, Bo gestured at Túathal, who stared blankly at his hand, then looked wildly around.

'The flask,' Brenna hissed. Túathal shook his head, the word unfamiliar.

'It's next to my bag,' Bo said. There was no hint of exasperation or urgency in his voice now. 'The gourd. That bulbous thing on its side.'

Túathal snatched the flask up. Water sloshed hollowly inside. He

199

leaned forward to offer it to Fiadh, but Bo gently intercepted him, uncapping the flask and holding it to Fiadh's parched lips.

'This is just water, Fiadh. Drink. Gently now. Do you know where you are?'

'It's dark… it's night.'

Túathal laughed, almost hysterical with relief. Brenna let out a sobbing sigh.

'Yes,' Bo agreed. 'Fiadh, where are you?'

Fiadh tried to shake her head. 'Where is it?' she moaned. She screwed her eyes shut. 'Where is the wolf? It's stronger, it – ow, it hurts!'

'It's gone, Fiadh,' Túathal cried, kneeling beside her. He cupped her face in his hands, ignoring Bo's protests. 'The wolf is dead. It's gone. You're free of it, Fiadh!' He glanced up at Brenna and grinned. 'Brenna freed you of it. Isn't that—'

Fiadh wailed. A howl of shock and utter grief.

Túathal flinched. He glanced from Brenna to Bo, mouthing wordless confusion. Bo shoved him aside. 'Fiadh, it's all right. You're all right.'

She shook her head. The shadows on her bandages darkened. Brenna cried out in alarm and tried to still her.

'The wolf's dead,' Fiadh gasped, her chest rising and falling rapidly. Her pupils almost swallowed up the violet of her irises. 'I can't live without it. Oh, *Pabbi*, oh, it *hurts!* I'm not strong enough!'

'I'm sorry!' Brenna burst out. 'Fiadh, I'm sorry! It was me. I killed it, I burned you. I didn't – I didn't mean to hurt you!'

'Stop.' Túathal was on his hands and knees, staring from one to the other. Bo put out a restraining arm, but he batted it away. He clasped Brenna's shoulder and caught Fiadh's fluttering hand. 'Fiadh, what are you talking about? Brenna freed you from that wolf. You wanted to be rid of it. Remember?'

'No, you don't – I wanted to *control* it!'

'No,' Túathal persisted. 'I remember. When I… when I held you back that night…' He grimaced, as if in physical pain. 'It made you hurt people, and – oh, Fiadh, you have such a gentle heart. You couldn't live with that. Because you *aren't* a monster. If only my heart were so gentle.'

Her eyes found his. Wild and afflicted. He fought to hold them, with warmth and tenderness. Unlike before, when he'd clung to her with bitterness and cold wrath. The frenzied edge in her eyes softened as she gazed up at him.

'The wolf won't hurt anyone again,' he murmured.

Tears welled in her eyes and spilled into her hair. 'No, Túathal. My heart isn't as gentle as you think. Even though I knew the damage it did, that *I* did, I couldn't want it to be gone. In my heart, I clung to it. It made me stronger. How awful am I?'

'I don't believe that.'

Fiadh frowned. She tilted her head back and for the first time saw Brenna's face bent over her. She let out a little gasp. 'Brenna…'

Brenna smiled and touched Fiadh's cheek. 'When I first saw you, you recognised me. You knew the wolf had attacked me. And it broke your heart. Oh, I believe you were conflicted.' Her fingers brushed Fiadh's bandaged shoulder. 'Strength. Freedom to escape and go where you like. I understand why you wouldn't want to give those up.'

'But you did, Fiadh,' Túathal insisted. He squeezed her hand. 'At least a part of you longed for freedom *from* that fierce strength. That's why you came to me.' He hung his head. 'And I let you down.'

Brenna touched his hand. 'We both did. Can you forgive us?'

Fiadh looked from one face to the other. From sister to brother and back. 'Brenna. Túathal. You're here. Together.'

'My mother was hers too.' Túathal cocked his head. 'You knew?'

'I guessed.'

Brenna bent and kissed Fiadh's damp forehead. 'You brought us together, Fiadh.' Túathal nodded, a grin breaking over his face.

Fiadh opened her mouth, then closed it, unable to speak through lips that quavered with emotion. She swallowed and finally managed to whisper, 'Is there anything to forgive?'

'Plenty,' Bo said dryly from behind them. Túathal peered over his shoulder at the young man. He was leaning back on his hands, his eyebrows raised. 'But I think this is quite enough for one night.' He smiled at Fiadh, ignoring her visible confusion. 'You need to rest.'

'Night…' Fiadh repeated. She let go of Túathal's hand and started to push herself up. Túathal exclaimed and Brenna touched her arm to restrain her. But Fiadh shook her head. 'Please. Let me see.'

Túathal exchanged a look with Brenna. 'See what?'

'The sky. Please.'

'Why?' Brenna demanded. 'Bo just said—'

'All right.'

'Bo!'

'Just a couple of minutes. Help her up. Túathal?'

'I can carry her…'

'Up there,' Fiadh begged, gesturing at the tower door. They stared at her. Brenna opened her mouth to argue, but Fiadh gripped her wrist and looked up beseechingly. 'Please!'

Túathal hesitated, but when Bo nodded, he took her up in his arms, blankets and all. Although he tried to be gentle, he could see that every step, every slight movement pained her.

Fiadh screwed her eyes shut. Her good hand clawed at the hood of his garment and she pressed her face into the fur. She didn't raise her head as he carried her up the spiralling stairs. Brenna went before him and he heard the sound of Bo's sedated footsteps behind.

⌘

Fiadh felt a cool wind on her face.

Túathal had stopped. She knew where they must be. Letting out her pent-up breath, she turned her head and raised her eyes to the heavens. To a canopy of winking lights. Her eyes widened in wonder at the glitter-black expanse above, arching over the ocean to the horizon. The moon's pale light scattered over the sea, painting its frothy caps silver.

'Stars,' she breathed softly, so the others wouldn't hear her voice above the wind and the crash of waves. 'I remember them, *Pabbi*.'

She was small, frail. Too light without the weight of the wolf's pelt on her shoulders.

She breathed in deeply through her nose but smelled only a dull impression of salt sea. She would miss it. She saw days ahead when she would miss its power, its speed, even its savagery, deeply enough to ache.

But if she could face the night without trepidation, without fear at what she would do, who she would hurt – if she could wake without the taste of blood on her teeth, if she could see nights and stars with her own eyes… she could make peace with it.

She would learn to live without the wolf's pelt. Learn to live again in her own skin.

SUNLIGHT poured unfiltered through the scullery's newly cleaned windows. Sweat beaded on Brenna's brow as she scrubbed the counter, a bucket of snowmelt at her elbow. The slate floor gleamed and the mid-morning light traced hitherto-forgotten threads of blue and red in the beaten hearthrug. With every day of cleaning, of sweeping cobwebs from the rafters and sanding the scored doors, of clearing shards of glass and crystal from the lantern room, the lighthouse seemed to fade back in time. Fade back into the home she remembered from her childhood.

And she hated it.

A couple of days after Fiadh had woken, they'd restored the mattress to the bedframe. Fiadh had slept most of the day and night, almost comatose, and at first it'd made Brenna anxious. When she'd raised her concerns with Túathal and Bo, however, the selkie had pointed out that as the wolf had taken over Fiadh's body through the night, she was simply catching up on months of sleep. Bo had attended to her daily, sneaking food and firewood over when he could.

He'd taken Brenna's clothes from the night she'd been arrested, torn them to tatters, doused them in sheep's blood he'd traded from the butcher, and scattered them on the fringes of the wood. Later, he'd brought the news that watchmen had found the scraps and called off the search. The prevailing rumour was that the feywalkers, those agents of the natural order, had reckoned their judgement after all.

Yet still, here she was. A prisoner in the lighthouse again. She hunched her shoulders and attacked the stains on the counter with a frustrated ferocity they didn't deserve.

Túathal was upstairs, in the lantern room. She sensed he was as restless as she was, as tense as she was.

'At least *you* can go outside,' she'd snapped the other day. He'd turned doleful eyes on her and shaken his head.

'If I go,' he'd said, 'I will go to the water's edge. If I go to the water's edge, I will step into the lapping tide. If I step into the tide and feel it drawing me in and calling me home, I won't be able to resist it. And if I am unable to resist it, I'm afraid I will leave you, sister.'

So instead, he stood on the balcony, hands tight around the rail, staring out at the ocean with silent longing. A prisoner, bound only by quiet obligation. Or maybe, if Brenna could dare to dream, he was bound to the lighthouse by a small, budding love. The simple love of a brother for a sister.

Brenna groaned and swiped a hand across her sweaty brow. She tucked a loose strand of hair behind her ear. Leaned across the counter, unlatched the window, and shoved it open. Hefted the bucket of dirty water to the sill and tipped it onto the muddy earth below. Tugged the window closed and wrestled with the latch until it clicked. Dropped her scrubbing brush into the bucket and deposited it in a nook beneath the counter. Sighing, she turned around.

Fiadh was swinging her legs off the bed and standing up. She had Brenna's dusky purple cloak draped over her shoulders, holding it together at her collar with one bandaged hand. Her legs were bare. She'd spent so long alone, in wolf hide, that she was still unused to clothes.

'What's the matter, Brenna?' she asked softly.

'Should you be getting up?' Brenna deflected, crossing the room.

Fiadh gave her a small smile. 'My legs are fine. As long as I'm careful and don't stress the wound, Bo said it's okay to move around.' Her smile faded. 'Is Túathal's leg okay? The one I… it…'

'He hasn't said anything about it, so I expect it's healing fine.'

'And your bites?'

'Fiadh,' Brenna said severely, tilting the other girl's chin so she was forced to meet Brenna's steady eyes. 'My scars aren't your fault. Don't start blaming yourself again. If anything, it's those rotten townsfolk who are to blame.'

Fiadh nodded and tried to smile again. Setting her jaw, she walked shakily to the hearthrug. Brenna helped her lower herself to sit, as she turned her head slowly this way and that, taking in the polished slate, gleaming counter, and spotless mantelpiece.

'You've done a lot to fix this place up.'

'It's all I can do to keep myself sane,' Brenna sighed. 'I can't believe I'm stuck here again.'

They heard the stairs creak behind them and both turned to see Túathal. He had a faraway look about his face, hair falling in wind-tangled waves about his shoulders. Raising his eyes, he blinked at Fiadh. 'Aren't you meant to be resting?'

'And what about you? You shouldn't be walking up and down those stairs so often with… your injury.'

'It's the only thing keeping me sane.' Túathal limped over and lay down between them. Frowning, he stared up at the rafters. 'Or perhaps it's tossing me upon the rocks.'

'Hm?'

He rolled his head to look at Fiadh. 'I haven't seen her again,' he whispered. 'Not once.'

'Seen who?' Brenna rested her arms on her knees. She'd gleaned snatches of information about the selkies in the past few days, in particular that the young members of the clan had come to the crescent beach for their bridal season. Túathal had said he was the only one left. The others had returned to their islands about a week ago. 'Someone from your clan? Were you expecting them to look for you?'

Her half-brother shut his mouth with a muted *clop*, guiltily averting his eyes.

'What?'

'The lighthouse showed us memories, Brenna,' Fiadh murmured.

'What do you mean?'

Fiadh swept her eyes around the lighthouse's main room. 'It showed us visions, of your mother. How she lived here. How she… how she died.'

'Visions? The lighthouse showed you visions? Of my *mother?*' She stared from Túathal to Fiadh. What they were saying was almost unbelievable. But at the same time, things were slotting into place in the back of her mind. How they'd known so much about her, so much about her father and mother. She pressed a hand to her pounding head. 'Show me,' she said. 'Where—'

Fiadh reached for her arm and gave it a squeeze. 'I'm sorry, Brenna.' Her expression was kind, but helpless and sad. 'I haven't seen any visions since… the wolf's last night.'

Túathal pushed himself up and butted Brenna's shoulder. She fought the instinct to recoil at his touch. Her brother's way of showing affection was still unusual to her, but it was nice to have someone touch her with casual tenderness. It reminded her of her mother's touch. Tentatively, she patted Túathal's hair.

'I think I know why.'

The siblings looked up at Fiadh.

'What?' Brenna asked.

'When I first saw the visions, I thought… well, I thought the lighthouse was trying to show me how to get rid of my – the wolf pelt. I saw a woman, your mother, here in the lighthouse without a pelt, then on the beach with one. Among the selkies. But the visions didn't really have anything to do with me. They weren't *for* me. They were for you, both of you. They revealed what happened to her and brought you both together.' Fiadh tilted her head to the side and smiled a little apologetically. 'A son of the sea and a daughter of the lighthouse keeper, both children of one mother. And she was the reason the lighthouse was broken. Not directly. But when she… when she died and the tide raged against your father, Brenna, and against Sjavaba, the townspeople broke it.'

'We know all this,' Brenna said. 'What has it got to do with the lighthouse?'

'I think it just wants to be restored.' Fiadh drew the folds of the cloak more tightly around her. 'For years, it hasn't been able to do what it was made for, when it was most needed. Because of that...' Sighing, she bowed her head. 'Who knows how many people have suffered? How many have… have been killed?'

Túathal moved as if to hug her but stopped, remembered her wound. Instead, he gently touched her hand. She smiled gratefully.

'I don't understand.' Brenna leaned closer. 'The lighthouse hasn't been restored. I've tidied it up a bit, but it's still broken. It still doesn't work. You'd have to replace the globe and refill the fuel stores and tune up the mechanism. It's a big job.'

Fiadh raised her eyebrows, her violet eyes wide. 'Could you do it?'

'I'm sorry?'

'Could *you* restore it?'

A familiar ache cinched Brenna's chest. She shook her head sadly. 'No, Fiadh.' The other girl's hopeful glow faded, her shoulders slumping. 'I know how it works. I know how to fix it and I know how to keep it working. But I could never do it. For one thing, the people of Sjavaba would never accept it. Would never *allow* it. And I don't want to. I can barely stand being here right now. The only reason I'm still here is, well, I can't show my face in Sjavaba. And there's nowhere else for me to go.'

Túathal sat up straight. His face lit up with a grin. 'Yes, there is! You could come home with me, to our islands.'

At his words, Brenna's heart sang.

All at once, she was a small girl again. Her mother cradled her by the fire, singing a song in the language only they knew. Brenna could hear the words in her ears, as if her mother were singing them again, in a voice as rich and smooth as wild honey. A song of distant shores and dancing tribes, of hidden coves and silver tides. A song that throbbed with longing.

'No, I can't. Have you forgotten? Since my father incited the wrath of the tide, no ship has been able to sail in or out of Sjavaba. The waters are deadly and the storms are relentless. Even my father's death wasn't enough to satiate the sea.'

Fiadh gathered herself and stood. The cloak hissed on the slate as she crossed to the scullery. Warm sunshine spilled over her, strands of her cream hair turning gold in its light.

She touched the glass. With a click, the window swung open. A warm breeze sighed in. 'The storms have relented, Brenna,' she said softly, turning to look at her friends.

The son of the tide. The daughter of the keeper. Both children of the woman whose life the tide had sought to avenge. United at last.

'I don't think the tide will stop you leaving. I think... I think it's finally at peace.'

42

IN the early hours, when cold mist blew in from the bay and billowed lazily through Sjavaba's streets, two figures slipped through the breach in the walls. The angular-faced young man guided his companion, a girl draped in the folds of a purple cloak, over the rubble. They stole down the southern district's deserted paths, weaving around the mouldering remains of houses and workshops, warehouses and sheds. The young man's lantern cast a dirty yellow glow, barely piercing the grey.

Fiadh pinched the elbow of Bo's shirt, following his lead. Every now and then, she peeked up at his profile. She barely knew him, yet he'd been unwaveringly kind to her, to them all. Not only had he treated her wounds and stalled the watchmen from searching further for Brenna, he'd even bartered for a retired fisherman's discarded skiff and a coil of rope. When Brenna had voiced her decision, Bo had been eager to help.

'You were there, at the *apótekari's*,' Fiadh said, as Bo led her around a corner. He glanced at her sidelong.

'When the watchman brought a shivering wild thing to our door?' he replied dryly. But he smiled. 'Yes. That was me.'

'I didn't think Brenna had any friends.'

'She doesn't…' Trailing off, he slowed to a stop. 'Ah, we're here.'

Fiadh looked at the house they had stopped in front of. The top

210

two storeys had caved in on themselves, but the ground floor appeared to be intact. Bo pointed to the heavy wooden door with his chin and pulled Fiadh onto the doorstep.

Fiadh stood to one side. Bo drew the key Brenna had given him from his pocket and bent to unlock the door.

'Why are you helping her?' Fiadh asked, above the metallic rasp of the key in the lock. There was a muted click and Bo turned the knob, his long fingers ghostly against the dark wood. The door squealed inwards. Bo peered inside and held his lantern high. Satisfied, he crossed the threshold.

'You could call it a guilty conscience.' He set the lantern on Brenna's formidable table and edged around it to the bedchamber. 'Clothes and matches, wasn't it?'

'And any viable food,' Fiadh added. She opened the pantry doors to reveal a cache of clouded jars. Heavily favouring her burned arm, she moved them one by one to the tabletop. 'What did you do?'

Bo returned to the kitchen. He heaved an intricately carved clothes chest onto the table, thin arms straining with the weight. It clunked loudly as it struck the tabletop, which shuddered, the jars clinked together. He flipped the lid open and started piling the clothes into a canvas satchel.

'I turned my back on her. After the floods and the wrecks.'

Fiadh watched him carefully. His hands slowed in their work, his slender fingers trailing over the chest's carved surface.

'I was born in Sjavaba. On my mother's side, I'm a descendant of one of the Old Families, the same line as Eldress Orla. My father was a foreigner. He worked on a merchant ship. When he married, he brought his father, my *Afi*, to live with him here. He was at sea when the storms started. Terrible, monstrous storms.' Bo pinched the bridge of his nose and sniffed. 'My mother and grandmother were doing business on the docks when the waves struck.'

Fiadh wished she hadn't asked. Taking a basket from the pantry, she started packing the jars of pickled eggs and vegetables and fish into it. 'Did he die in the storms?'

Bo nodded. 'The tempest drove the wreck of his ship right into the old harbour.' He closed the chest and rounded the table to fetch the matches off the mantelpiece. 'My grandfather knew what Idunn – Brenna's mother – was. When he discovered she'd disappeared just before the storms…' He shook his head. 'They were convinced that the tide would be appeased if the keeper died. When the storms continued, we decided the curse must reside in Brenna herself.'

'In a way, it did.'

Bo shrugged. 'It's no excuse, though, is it? I blamed her for what happened to my family. I was the last one who could've stood by her, but I let them scorn her. *I* scorned her. But if I've been given another chance to be the friend I should've been all along…' He hefted the basket off the table and nestled it in the crook of his elbow. 'I'd have to be quite the petty ass not to take it.'

⌘

Fiadh and Bo found the fisherman's old skiff resting on its side, half-under the rotting boardwalk, wedged between its barnacle-encrusted pylons. Bo hauled it over the sand, with much cursing, until its nose slid into the quietly lapping tide. They nestled the basket of jars and the satchel of clothes into the bottom of the skiff, mist coiling about them as they moved.

Squinting, Fiadh looked to the east. The lighthouse hill's bulky shadow loomed behind the thinning fog. She followed the line of the cliff down to where it met the low tide.

'See Silver yet?'

'No… have you tied—'

'Doing it now.' He knotted one end of the rope he'd bought off the fisherman through a ring at the bow of the skiff. 'Hope this holds,' he muttered.

'Did your father teach you to tie knots?'

Bo cocked an eyebrow with an air of condescension. 'My father was a translator and an appraiser of valuables, not a sailor.' He held out a hand to Fiadh and helped her into the skiff. They waited a few more minutes, the grey morning lightening into a soft peach-pink with the rising sun. As the mist faded, Fiadh saw a whiskered face bob above the low rolling waves, a stone's throw away.

'There he is.'

Bo put his hands on his hips, eyes widening in uncharacteristic awe. Fiadh smiled and leaned forward, resting her arms on the prow. For a beat, she almost opened her mouth to sing to Túathal. To call him to the shore, as she'd witnessed on the night they'd met. When the water brides had asked their grooms to love them and hold them and dance with them until the stars fell from the heavens.

She blinked, catching her breath. Pressed a hand to her chest and felt her heart flutter.

Túathal shook his hood free. His form melted, seal to man. He waded towards them, disturbing the water so it swirled about his waist, his thighs, his knees, his calves in white foaming tendrils. Stopping in front of the skiff's bow, he grinned down at Fiadh, seated on the front bench. His liquid eyes, framed by long sea-wet lashes, stirred a yet nameless emotion in her breast.

The skiff rocked as Bo clambered in behind her. Túathal nodded at him, took hold of the rope, and drew them out into the water. After tying it around his torso, he sank back into the shallows, drawing his hood over his head. The skiff bucked a little in the breakers, but soon it was skimming over the calm swells. Fiadh let her breath sigh through her teeth and gripped the sides.

Túathal guided the skiff around the bluff, expertly avoiding the rocks that jutted out of the water like cruel teeth. As they rounded the outcrop and glided closer to the crescent beach, Fiadh saw a flicker of red against the black basalt of the cliffs. She raised a hand. Brenna, growing bigger as they neared the shore, waved both arms in acknowledgement.

Feeling the skiff slow, Fiadh looked down. Túathal's shadow

circled to the back of the boat. His head broke the surface, his hood slipping back, and he braced his arms against the stern, pushing the skiff the last few metres to shore. The prow crunched onto the glitter-black sand. Brenna ran towards them and helped Fiadh up out of the skiff. 'How did you go?' she asked. 'Did you – oh, that's great! Thank you.'

'You're lively,' Bo drawled. He lifted his leg over the side and swore as the boat pitched under him. Túathal caught his arms just in time to stop him falling into the water, and laughed, a joyful, infectious sound. Fiadh chuckled. Covered her mouth, hiding the way her lips quavered even as she giggled. Because this was goodbye.

Clapping her hands, Brenna laughed. Bo rolled his eyes at her and strode up the sands with as much dignity as he could muster. 'Was never one for boats,' he muttered. '*You've* never sailed in one either.'

Brenna shook her head, curly mane flaring. 'No. But I've dreamed of this since I was a little girl.' She kicked off her boots and dropped them into the bottom of the boat. Flashing Bo and Fiadh a fierce grin, she leapt into the wash of the tide. Shrieked in delight as the icy foam broke and swept over her bare feet. Clutched at Túathal's waiting arms, gripped them so tight her nails bit into his skin. And there was a catch in her voice when she spoke. 'Will your people accept me?'

Túathal beamed. '*Our* people,' he said. 'Why shouldn't they? You're our clan's long-lost daughter. Pa will be excited to meet you.'

Brenna snorted in disbelief. 'Excited?'

'Yes! He'll want to know all about you, and tell you how much you remind him of our mother. Your spirit, your zeal, your love for a world you've yearned for but not yet explored…' He pressed his forehead to hers. 'He's going to love you, Brenna!'

Laughter spilled from Brenna's lips. She hugged him, then spun around, kicking up water. Leapt back up the sand to where Bo and Fiadh stood. Breathless, as if she'd been running. She looked up at Bo first and shrugged helplessly. 'I don't know what to say, Bo.'

Bo smirked. 'Take care, bastard?' he suggested with a shrug.

'Don't damage the lighthouse further than it already is?'

Brenna scoffed. 'You're not as much of a bastard as you make out. And, seriously, are you sure? It's an exhausting, isolating job. Did you really understand what I told you about the mechanism and how it all works?'

He rolled his eyes. 'Yes, yes, you've made it abundantly clear I'll be breaking my back and going insane, and I'll deserve most of it. I *am* sure. But don't think I'm making a life commitment – I have my grandfather's ancient medical traditions to learn and uphold. Once ships start coming back to Sjavaba, I'll find my replacement. Are we dandy?'

'Yes. We're good.' She held out a hand to him. He gave her a subdued smile and shook it.

'Godspeed, Brenna. I hope you find a place and a people you can call home.'

Brenna blinked. She pressed her lips together and nodded. 'Thanks, Bo.'

Fiadh swallowed. Her turn now.

Túathal seemed to have felt it too. Dropping the rope, he strode out of the water to stand with Brenna. She let go of Bo's hand and turned to Fiadh.

'Fiadh,' she said, a catch in her voice. 'I – I…' She shook her head. 'Ha, again. I don't know what to – thank you. Thank you *so* much.' She wrapped her arms around Fiadh, as carefully as she might embrace a figure of delicate glass. Then her arms tightened. 'Come with us,' she pleaded fervently. Leaning back, she fixed Fiadh with her honey-brown eyes. 'Why don't you come with us?'

'Yes!' Túathal reached out and touched Fiadh's cheek. 'Come with us to our islands. Dula would love to see you again and Quillen will come to understand. The islands are beautiful. There are sea caves that shine with iridescent light and brooks that bubble up out of the land, fields of wild grasses and hidden coves…'

For a moment, Fiadh dared to dream of such a life. She saw

herself step into the boat behind Brenna to be drawn across the placated sea. Heard the echoes of selkie songs, the stamp and clap of their dances. Smelled their sea-salt scent thick in the air. Could almost feel the velvet-soft fur of their pelts at her fingertips.

'You can't know how much I long to.'

'Then *do*,' Brenna urged.

Fiadh shook her head. 'I'm free, at last. The wolf is gone. How can I learn to live without it if I come with you? If I'm reminded every day of what I've lost? No. You were born to your skin, Túathal. And Brenna, they're your people. If I came with you, I might resent you. I might… steal from you.'

She drew the folds of her cloak more tightly around her shoulders. 'Besides, I made a promise to my father. But…' Her lips trembled. 'I'm going to miss you. Both of you. So, *so* much.' She flung her arms around their necks, ignoring the pain that lanced through her arm and back. It was nothing. Túathal and Brenna's arms folded around her.

'Me too,' Brenna said, her voice stiff with unshed emotion. 'Fiadh, you better take care of yourself!'

'I don't want to leave you,' Túathal cried, squeezing her tight. 'I don't want this to be goodbye.'

'Oh, Túathal. You should know better than anyone,' Fiadh chided gently. 'The tide goes out, but always comes back in. The moon is like that too. It wanes, but always, *always* waxes full again.' She looked between them, seeing the intensity in their wide eyes. She felt the same intensity in her own chest.

'So, we will say goodbye,' she whispered, her words misting soft in the air. 'But when the time comes, I believe we'll meet again.'

She kissed Brenna's tawny-freckled cheek and the fawn patch smeared across Túathal's jaw, rising on tiptoe just to reach.

'Go,' she gasped, releasing them. Túathal tried to grab hold of her hand, as if she'd disappear with the fading mist. Brenna opened her mouth to protest. But Fiadh pushed them gently away.

The sun burst on the horizon, warm on her skin, flooding the beach with honeyed light that turned the black sand to bronze and the tide to gold.

'Be bold. Be glad. We will see each other again. Go!'

And Fiadh was smiling through her tears.

ACKNOWLEDGMENTS

Above all, my thanks and praise go to God, the Author of Life, my Father, Saviour, and King. Thank you for my love of words and stories, and for the seasons you have given me to practise and cultivate this gift. I hope to tell many more stories, to your glory. Amen.

I am so fortunate to have had the endless support of my family throughout this journey. To my parents, Darrell and Margaret, thank you for your loving encouragement in everything, especially my writing aspirations. To Aunty Carolyn, I'm so grateful for your generosity, particularly in sharing your home with me while I took a year to write. It was such a blessing to have the freedom to pursue this dream. And to my brothers and sister, Luke, Josh, and Zoë, I appreciate your assurances that you definitely will finish reading *Moontide* when it's published. Thanks guys.

It was very special to share my writing wins and woes, concept sketches and milestones with my besties and beta readers, Abbie, Cara, and Amelia. Love you, girls! And to everyone who asked about my writing and my progress, helped me navigate my publishing queries, shared in my anticipation, and celebrated my successes, thank you.

Finally, I want to thank the Hawkeye Publishing team. From the insightful feedback of the Hawkeye Manuscript Development Prize judges to my editors' diligent efforts to hone my words, I trust that they truly care about making *Moontide* the best it can be. Thank you for this opportunity and for all your patient help in guiding me through my first publishing adventure.

ABOUT THE AUTHOR

Mary Greenwood has been an aspiring writer and hungry reader since her primary school years. She has a long-standing love of language, stories and art, leading her to study linguistics and ancient history, as well as to practise archery, fencing, drawing, and embroidery. When she's not at work or daydreaming about her next writing project, she may be plotting or participating in a Dungeons and Dragons campaign.

Book reviews can make or break a book. If you liked what you read today,
please do consider posting a review on Goodreads or your favourite forum.

Moontide is available at **www.hawkeyebooks.com.au**
and all good bookstores and libraries.